D1010546

-28-99   *Date*

how I spent my last night on earth

Todd Strasser

Simon & Schuster
Books for Young Readers

To Lia and Geoff,
my favorite mysteries,
with oceans of love

Simon & Schuster Books for Young Readers

 An imprint of Simon & Schuster Children's Publishing Division
1230 Avenue of the Americas, New York, New York 10020

Text copyright © 1998 by Todd Strasser. All rights reserved including the right of reproduction in whole or in part in any form. SIMON & SCHUSTER BOOKS FOR YOUNG READERS is a trademark of Simon & Schuster. Book design by Heather Wood. The text for this book is set in Breughel. Printed and bound in the United States of America.
First Edition 10 9 8 7 6 5 4 3 2 1

Library of Congress Cataloging-in-Publication Data Strasser, Todd. How I spent my last night on Earth / by Todd Strasser. p.   cm.   Summary: When a rumor appears on the Internet that a giant asteroid is about to destroy Earth, Legs Hanover scrambles to meet the boy of her dreams, elusive Andros Bliss. ISBN 0-689-81113-6 [1. High schools—Fiction. 2. Schools—Fiction.] I. Title. PZ7.S899Hr 1998   [Fic]—dc21   97-43473
CIP   AC

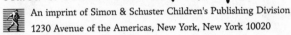

FIRST
F
EDITION

Excerpt from "It's the End of the World As We Know It," by William Berry, Peter Buck, Michael Mills and John Stipe © 1989 Night Garden Music (BMI). All Rights administered by Warner-Tamerlane Publishing Corp. (BMI). All Rights Reserved. Used by Permission. Warner Bros. Publications US Inc., Miami, FL 33014

OTHER BOOKS BY TODD STRASSER
SET AT TIME ZONE HIGH:

How I Changed My Life

★

Girl Gives Birth
to Own Prom Date

paperback title:

How I Created My Perfect Prom Date

"IT'S THE END OF THE WORLD AS WE KNOW IT...
AND I FEEL FINE."

—R.E.M.

"THE SUPREME REALITY OF OUR TIME IS...
THE VULNERABILITY OF THIS PLANET."

—*John F. Kennedy*

The world may end tomorrow morning.

Everyone was talking about it at school today.

School—a universe unto itself.

Inhabited by teenagers. Who everyone says are in a world of their own anyway.

Maybe.

Derman said the news of the possible end of the world first appeared on the Internet around nine o'clock last night. I didn't hear about it because I'd turned off the phone and the television to cram for a monster Chinese test today.

Too bad.

Maybe if I'd known, I wouldn't have bothered to study.

No, that's not true. I would have studied anyway.

The first sign of something unusual this morning was

the state of the student parking lot at Timothy Zonin High.

The established cliques weren't collected in their usual tribal gathering places.

The burnouts weren't palming cigarettes over by the grease spots at the far end of the lot.

The wanna-bes weren't squeezed between parked cars, busy fixing each other's makeup.

The car nuts weren't huddled around someone's open hood, worshiping a new carburetor.

And finally, the jocks weren't ranging all over the parking lot, pumping testosterone and challenging everyone else's territorial rights in the guise of throwing a football.

Normally (if there is such a thing) each clique forms its own little planet.

Each planet has its own orbit.

It may be vaguely aware that the other cliques exist.

But it would never give a thought to crossing paths.

You know the picture.

But this morning everything was different.

The planets had left their orbits.

The cliques had burst apart, then come back together to form one huge milling liquid universe.

A great sea of unexpected interaction.

People you never saw together.

People you'd have sworn hated each other.

All of them together, talking.

I parked, but didn't get out of my car. Instead, I sat there watching, wondering if what they had was contagious.

* ★ *

A rapping sound on the window caught my attention. Outside was a hand balled into a fist, the sound caused by the repeated impact of a dull silver skull-shaped ring against the shatterproof glass.

My eyes followed the hand to the wrist covered with fine blond hairs, and from there to the worn brown leather sleeve of a jacket. The sleeve formed a right angle around a scraped red motorcycle helmet with two brown leather gloves tucked neatly into it. Then came a brown leather shoulder. Then a strong chin studded with two-day-old blond stubble, a thin Roman nose, and the piercing hazel green eyes of...Andros Bliss.

Andros Bliss?

Have you ever drifted off into fantasy and wondered what it would be like to be with a guy you could never in a million lifetimes conceive of yourself being with?

Normally, I don't.

I mean that I rarely if ever do.

Well, maybe once in a while, in some late afternoon study hall, in the fog of cerebral exhaustion, I've done it.

Actually, I do it rather often.

That is, daydream about The Totally Inappropriate Guy.

A guy who, you are reasonably sure, doesn't have the wherewithal to even know you exist.

Or if he does know you exist, he doesn't seem to care.

A guy who, you are absolutely certain, would break a girl's heart into a thousand pieces. Like so many shattered green glass crumbs at the intersection of Daydream Path and The Reality Super Expressway.

And he wouldn't even have the perspicacity to realize what he'd done.

Still, you're probably thinking, *Fess up already, girl. Who is this Andros Bliss?*

Who is this totally inappropriate male with whom you choose to dally in your foggy noneducational idylls?

This Andros Bliss who at that very moment was tapping his skull ring against my shatterproof window.

Andros with his wiry body and all-knowing ironic smile.

Andros, who was blond and rode an old, dented, scratched red motorcycle. Not like the glittery, graphically enhanced, low-slung beasts some boys bought in the spring and almost immediately crashed.

Andros, who came to school irregularly, especially when the surf was up.

Andros—to whom I'd never spoken a single word in my life.

Tapping on my shatterproof window.

My mind went uncharacteristically blank.

My heart raced. Goose bumps marched rapidly up the derma.

To be honest, I was somewhat aghast. Why was I reacting this way?

Just because I'd mused about him?

Just because, in a moment of mental fatigue, I'd dallied

in some romantic fantasy with his imaginary being?

What was I so frightened of?

They were my private fantasies, to which he could have no access.

The fact that he now stood outside my car window had to be pure coincidence.

He couldn't possibly know how I felt about him...

Could he?

Andros tapped again.

Despite my inexplicably intense physical reaction to his presence, decorum dictated a response.

In a light-headed dizziness I was utterly unaccustomed to, I reached for the hand crank and tried to roll down the window, completely forgetting that said window was inoperative.

Meanwhile, outside, Andros, the object of my daydreams, waited.

I'd like to pause here to explain a few things that may help put the absurdity of this situation into perspective.

First of all, I had a boyfriend.

All right, he wasn't *exactly* a boyfriend.

He was...more than a friend, but less than a boy.

No, no, no. That was a joke. He *was* a boy. His name, regretfully, was Derman Bloom.

It was some kind of family name.

He was very, very smart.

Derman and I had a very intimate relationship that stopped just short of anything physical. He openly acknowledged that he wished it could be more.

But I had a mental block.

You see, I firmly believe that high school is potty training for life.

You probably don't remember being potty trained, so let me remind you of what happened. You were three years old, and wearing a diaper. Life was going along swimmingly and you were happy as a clam.

Then one day, for absolutely no logical reason, your parents became obsessed with getting you to use the toilet.

At first you didn't understand what the big deal was about.

Then you started to understand—and immediately rebelled.

Finally, because your parents were bigger and stronger, and because you needed them for all sorts of stuff, you acquiesced and learned to use the toilet.

After that, things weren't so bad.

Your parents were thrilled, and you felt pretty good too.

In fact, it was hard to believe that you ever used a diaper in the first place.

That's what I mean when I say that high school is potty training for life.

Only, the toilet is college.

I say that only in the most positive way.

College is where we're supposed to go.

Just like the toilet.

And when we do it, it makes our parents incredibly happy, and is good for us too (better job possibilities and no more diaper rash!).

So, getting back to poor Derman and my mental block. Since to me high school was nothing more than a peculiar intermediate step toward real life, just like toilet training, I would never think of doing anything *serious* during it.

Which left poor Derman feeling awfully frustrated.

But he seemed to deal with it.

Now, completing the circle back to Andros and the absurdity of the situation...

Besides that fact that I had Derman, who performed all the functions of a male companion most suitably, I would, in roughly six months, be going to college in some faraway place.

And when I did, high school and everything *in* it would disappear and be forever forgotten.

Just like my diaper and, I would assume, Andros.

However, at that moment in the student parking lot of Time Zone High, in the newly liquid universe where cliques no longer seemed to exist, Andros was very real and extremely difficult to ignore.

Remembering finally that my car window did not work, I managed to open the door.

As I pushed it outward, I forced Andros to take a step back, thus pinning him against Dave Ignazzi's car in the spot next to mine.

"Oh, God, I'm really sorry." I was all aflutter as I looked up at him through the narrow gap between car and door. "I should have gotten the window fixed a long time ago. It's just...well...did you want something?"

Still pinned between my door and Dave Ignazzi's car, Andros fixed me with those intense hazel green eyes and said, "Do you know that the world may end tomorrow morning?"

✶ ✶ ✶

Time out.

I may have only been a high-school senior in the later stages of potty training for real life, but I'd already heard more than my fair share of ridiculous pickup lines. For example:

"If you were a McDonald's hamburger they'd call you McGorgeous." Or, *"You must be Jamaican because Jamaican me crazy."*

One tends to hear lines like that when one is a stunning auburn-haired beauty with a devastatingly well-proportioned figure.

You don't think I'm referring to me, do you?

I only wish...

I'm talking about my dear friend Angie Sunberg.

She's the beauty with the great body.

I'm okay, mind you. (The last pickup line anyone tried on me was *"Sure I'm missing some teeth, but that just makes more room for your tongue."* Yuck!)

Anyway, in my experience as Angie's friend, these pickup lines usually came from college guys at the beach, or worse—from men who looked like they must be married.

Angie ignored them and, often for the benefit of her friends, even pretended to be repulsed (sometimes one doesn't have to pretend).

But no one in recent memory had started a conversation with Angie or me by suggesting that the world might end the next morning.

I replied with, "You don't say."

The faint lines in Andros's high forehead bunched up. "You didn't hear about it?"

Naturally, I assumed I was being kidded. Wouldn't you

assume the same if someone you'd never spoken to came up and said something so completely outrageous?

I cheekily countered with, "Must've missed it."

"It's been all over the Internet since last night," Andros informed me with stone cold seriousness. "And the TV and radio."

I was truly puzzled. Why was Andros Bliss doing this? What was he trying to accomplish?

"I'm really sorry," I said, "but *what* are you talking about?"

"The world may end," Andros, still pinned between cars, repeated with frightening intensity. "There's this asteroid. On a collision course with the earth. And if it hits us, we're splat."

Splat?

Only then did it occur to me that he might actually be serious. I pulled the car door back a little, allowing him to slide out of the way. Then I got out and looked again at the liquid milling humanity around us.

Only now I saw the subtle deviations from the norm that I'd missed before.

The tear-streaked makeup and reddened eyes of the blubbering wanna-bes.

The grim, ashen looks on the faces of the jocks.

The feverishly smoking burnouts. Then again, they *always* looked like the world was going to end tomorrow, so that was nothing new.

I turned back to Andros. The blond stubble of his chin. The haunting, hazel green eyes—

When our gazes met, I felt the unfamiliar tremor

of being near someone I secretly desired.

But there were larger issues at stake. Such as the future of the human race.

"You're serious?" I asked.

He nodded.

I was struck at that moment by the irony of life. Here I was, finally speaking to Andros Bliss, guy of my dreams. And what did he say?

The world was about to end.

Talk about bad timing.

"Legs?" Coming toward us through the parking lot was Angie Sunberg, my ravishing, sexy, happy-go-lucky party-girl friend.

Her usually sparkling eyes were red rimmed.

Her normally bouncy reddish-brown hair hung limp.

Most shockingly, she wasn't wearing makeup!

Angie glanced at Andros with just a nanosecond's worth of a scowl. "I'm really sorry. Could you excuse us for a second?"

Andros took a step back.

Angie turned to me. "Can you believe it? Is this the worst?"

We flew into each other's arms and started to cry. To be honest, I hadn't even thought of crying until I saw her. It's not among my usual repertoire of responses. And despite the preponderance of evidence in the parking lot, I still found the whole idea of the end of the world pretty hard to swallow.

But crying, like yawning, tends to be contagious. Besides, Angie was my dearest friend, and you really hate to see friends cry by themselves.

Our sobbing was heartfelt but short. Then, sniffling and wiping tears off my cheek, I turned to look for Andros.

But he was gone.

REALITY:
1. THE STATE OR QUALITY OF BEING REAL
2. RESEMBLANCE TO WHAT IS REAL
—*Webster's Ninth New Collegiate Dictionary*

"What was that all about?" Angie asked, dabbing her eyes with her sleeve.

"You got me," I replied.

"I've seen him around," Angie said. "The handsome and mysterious type."

And no doubt destined to remain that way, I thought with disappointed resignation. "Are you okay?"

Angie shook her head and yawned. Dark rings circled her eyes. She looked almost ghostly.

"Didn't get much sleep last night?" I guessed.

It wasn't a particularly cold day, but she hugged herself and shivered. "I still can't believe it."

"Neither can I," I agreed wholeheartedly, since I still *didn't* believe it.

"No, not that," she said.

"Not what?" I asked, not understanding.

"Not the asteroid."

"Then what?"

"Something worse," Angie said.

The school bell rang. As if they had little minds of their own, my feet automatically started toward the entrance. The rest of my body followed, my mind completely distracted by these utterly unlikely developments.

What could be worse than impending global death and destruction?

I couldn't imagine.

And Angie wasn't prone to excessive drama. She was a sensible, intelligent girl who believed that our main purpose in life was to have fun, look great, and party down.

The next thing I knew, we passed through the front doors and went inside school.

The halls were in a tizzy. All around us people seemed directionless, like ants whose burrow has been flooded by mischievous boys with a hose.

People talking frantically.

People stumbling along in stunned muteness.

People crying.

People wondering out loud what to do.

Still on autopilot, Angie and I made our way through the crowd. Until, a dozen feet away, I saw Andros Bliss beside his open locker.

I stopped and stared.

He must have felt my gaze.

Our eyes locked.

I felt a warm nervous tingle spread through me.

"You're not mad at me, are you?" Angie asked.

"Sorry?" I turned away from Andros and looked at her.

"That I haven't told you what I'm wigged out about," she explained. "I want to tell you. Really, I *will* tell you. Just not right now. Are you mad?"

"I don't think so," I answered, feeling uncertain regarding just about everything at that moment. I glanced up the hall toward Andros's locker.

But once again he was gone.

An announcement came over the loudspeaker ordering the entire school to proceed immediately to the auditorium for an emergency assembly.

Angie and I shared a puzzled look. We'd never heard of such a thing.

Suddenly the directionless crowd had direction. We flowed down the hall like so many red blood cells coursing through the veins of interrupted education. Angie and I walked arm in arm in the jostle. United against the possibility of impending chaos and destruction. Behind us walked the inseparable triad of "Designated" Dave Ignazzi, Ray Neely, and Chase Hammond.

"Why'd we even bother coming to school?" Dave asked.

"Because they say there's only a *50* percent chance we're gonna be wiped out," Chase answered.

"Besides, what else would we do?" asked Ray.

"I know what I'd do," Dave answered with an insinuating snicker.

"With who?" asked Chase.

"With *what's* more like it," added Ray.

"Drop dead," Dave muttered.

"Soon enough," Ray replied.

The auditorium was crowded, and the cacophony of loud voices bordered on painful.

Maybe Dave Ignazzi was right. If the news was true, it was sort of odd that so many of our compatriots had bothered to come to school.

If life really was in danger of ending, why hadn't more people skipped?

Was it because they didn't have anything better to do?

Or did they come to school hoping to hear some kind of earth-shattering (oops!) news?

After all, wasn't school the chief authority in our lives?

What a depressing thought.

Angie and I stood near the back of the auditorium and scoped the crowd. I spotted Andros near the front, still wearing his brown motorcycle jacket and carrying his scraped helmet with the gloves in it. His rough-edged neatness was appealing. Thinking back to the school parking lot, I wondered if I could have made more of our first and only conversation.

No, considering the situation I couldn't blame myself for coming up short. And yet, it could have been so much more—

Wait!

Make more of my conversation with Andros?

With what end in mind?

Especially when *The End* (of the world) might be upon us.

Meanwhile Angie seemed distracted, scanning the crowd in an edgy manner that was unlike her.

"Who are you looking for?" I asked.

She gave me a helpless shrug.

"Can't say?" I guessed.

"I know I'm being totally obnoxious and I'm a million times sorry," she apologized, then covered her mouth with her hand and yawned.

"But it's not because of the alleged asteroid?" I asked, still puzzled.

"Well, it is...and it isn't," she answered. Then off my confused look she added, "It'll all make sense when I tell you."

"And when will that be?" I asked.

"Soon."

"Given the current state of things, will soon be soon enough?" I asked.

Angie smiled weakly.

Waiting for the assembly to begin, my thoughts began to drift, as they're wont to do when killing time.

Killing time.

Isn't it strange how words like *death* and *killing* and *murder* flit in and out of our everyday speech as innocently and barely noticeable as TV ads for detergent?

And yet, it's *DEATH!*

The most momentous thing in life.

How's that for a strange turn of a phrase?

Death...Life...

In the 1800s the British philosopher Jeremy Bentham

left instructions in his will to have his body stuffed. For years afterward his stuffed body was placed in a chair so that he could attend the annual meeting of the Royal Philosophical Society.

More recently, in Moscow a four-year-old girl lived with her dead mother for three weeks in their apartment. The girl survived on raw macaroni and water until a foul smell from the apartment prompted neighbors to call the police.

The Russian police explained that the girl "was not familiar with the concept of death." She thought her mother, who died in bed, was asleep. When asked about it, the girl said that her mother "got less pretty."

It occurred to me that if a giant asteroid really were to strike the earth, we would all get a lot less pretty.

Angie nudged me with her elbow. "So what do you think this assembly is about?"

"Career opportunities?" I quipped.

"Maybe temporary jobs," Angie suggested with a quick grin, reminding me of the old Angie.

Mr. Rope, esteemed assistant principal, stepped onto the stage. AV pervert Karl Luckowsky, looking unnaturally somber, handed him a microphone.

"All right, everyone, let's be seated," said Mr. Rope.

As usual, the masses were slow to respond.

"Come on, we're wasting time," Mr. Rope said impatiently.

"So?" someone shouted.

"What does it matter?" shouted someone else.

"I will not tolerate insubordination," Mr. Rope growled.

"What're you gonna do?" came the response. "Suspend us?"

The auditorium rippled with nervous laughter.

"Yes, I will," Mr. Rope replied when the laughter began to fade.

Loud derogatory murmurs started to run through the crowd.

"I get the feeling that when faced with a 50 percent chance of death, the threat of suspension doesn't pack much wallop," Angie observed.

But Mr. Rope would not be deterred. "Look, everyone," he said, "if you're not going to listen, why'd you bother to come to the assembly?"

The crowd fell into a stunned silence. As if we couldn't believe what we'd just heard.

Granted the news (if true) of a killer asteroid speeding toward the earth was shocking.

But this had to be the *second* most shocking thing that had happened so far that day.

"He *reasoned* with us!" Angie gasped. "I can't believe it! He spoke to us like we were adults. He even used *logic!*"

All around us, shocked students began to sit down.

"I can go peacefully to my grave now," Angie whispered.

"Not funny, given the circumstances," I whispered back.

Maybe we shouldn't have been surprised by the behavior of our assistant principal.

Not if I understood chaos theory correctly.

Even though chaos implies disorder on one level, it often gives rise to order on another.

It's all fractals and things.

Was it possible that we'd just had a demonstration of chaos theory right there in our very own auditorium?

Up on the stage, Mr. Rope looked as stunned as we felt.

He brought the microphone to his lips. "How come you had to wait until the end of the world to do that?"

A smattering of murmurs began to ferment in the crowd.

"No, no, stop!" Mr. Rope held out his hand. "Don't start talking. I want to savor this."

A moment of something close to silence passed. Then our assistant principal cleared his throat. "All right, ladies and gentlemen, I assume you are aware of the reports that a huge asteroid is on a collision course with the earth. The important thing to remember is that *nothing* has been officially confirmed."

Down in the front of the auditorium a thin pale hand went up.

I felt a mild jolt as I realized whose hand it was.

Alice Hackett's.

Alice was my friend.

An actress in school plays and a computer maven.

Pale skinned, jet black hair, eyes blackened with mascara.

Emotionally as fragile as cigarette ash.

Obsessed with death.

As best as I could recall, this was the first time she had ever raised her hand.

"Yes, Alice?" Mr. Rope said from the stage.

She stood up. "How can you say it's not confirmed? It's all over the Internet, Mr. Rope. It's been on TV and the radio."

"Hold on a minute," our assistant principal replied. "The only thing that's been reported on radio and television is the fact—wait, I don't want to use the word *fact,* because it's not a fact—the only thing that's been reported on television and radio is the *existence* of this rumor on the Internet. That's all. You have to remember, Alice, that *anyone* can get on the Internet and post anything they want."

But Alice would not be deterred. "What about the reports that the government knows about the asteroid, but they won't confirm it because they're afraid of riots?"

Mr. Rope seemed to bristle. "I won't vouch for the government, and I can't swear to you that they're not capable of lying or covering up. My brother was killed by friendly fire in Vietnam and it took the army *twenty-five* years to admit it. During Watergate we witnessed a *full-fledged* conspiracy at the *highest levels* of government. We watched the president of the United States get on television and outright *lie* to the people of this country."

Mr. Rope was clearly bent out of shape. His face was flushed and he paused to loosen his tie. "We know that the CIA has funded covert activities, *including* assassinations. We know they have traded weapons with the enemy. We even know that they have withheld information vital to the health and welfare of the citizens of this country. So don't ask *me* to tell you they're not covering something up."

A shocked hush fell over the auditorium.

Even Mr. Rope looked a bit astonished at what he'd just unleashed.

"So, you're saying that the government really *could* be covering up this asteroid?" Alice asked.

Mr. Rope blinked. "Uh...well...no, I don't know. I mean, I don't *think* they are. Not in *this* case."

"But you just said you couldn't be sure," Alice pointed out.

Mr. Rope quickly glanced offstage, looking for help.

There are no real grown-ups in high school.

There are students like you and me.

And there are teachers.

Know what they say about teachers?

Those who can grow up, do.

Those who can't grow up, teach.

Those who can't teach, teach gym.

Those who can't teach gym become principals.

We all knew that Mr. Rope was looking offstage at the main act, Wild Bill Dixon, former gym teacher and now the principal of Timothy Zonin High. While we in the audience couldn't hear what was being said because the assistant principal had covered the microphone with his hand, it appeared that he was having a heated discussion. In fact, it definitely looked as if Mr. Rope was begging Wild Bill to take over the spotlight.

Angie gave me a terrified look. "What's going on?" she whispered.

Before I could answer, Wild Bill Dixon strode onto the

stage and gruffly snatched the microphone from Mr. Rope.

Our principal did not look happy as our assistant principal slunk offstage. But he faced us and puffed out his chest.

"All right, ladies and gentlemen," he said. "I can see by your silence that the seriousness of this moment hasn't been lost to you."

A few groans rose out of the audience. There was no platitude Wild Bill couldn't master.

"The reason for this assembly was to separate fact from fiction," Wild Bill went on, glaring offstage. "Mr. Rope was *supposed* to clear the air so that we all knew where we stood."

"Is it possible for this guy *not* to speak in clichés?" someone near us whispered loudly.

Down in front my friend Alice was still standing, as if she had become the spokesperson for the entire student body. "Mr. Dixon, do you know that in 1989 another large asteroid missed us by only six hours? Scientists weren't even *aware* of it until after it passed."

"Yes, Alice," Wild Bill replied rather caustically. "I guess we watched the same show on TV this morning."

"*That* asteroid was about half a mile in diameter," Alice went on. "On the TV this morning they said *this* one is three miles wide and weighs two hundred thousand tons. That means it's almost six times bigger."

"It's only an unconfirmed rumor," Wild Bill stressed.

"How could the government possibly confirm it?" Alice asked heatedly. "There'd be total mayhem."

Once again Wild Bill glared offstage, as if he was royally peeved that Mr. Rope had put him in this spot. Then he turned back to us.

"Okay, listen," our principal said with an air of resignation. "Just for argument's sake, let's pretend that the
rumor is true, okay? It still means there's only a *50 percent* chance of impact. Given that fact, I am asking all of
you to continue to attend classes."

"Why?" asked Alice.

Wild Bill looked exasperated. "Because you are *supposed* to. Because until this rumor is confirmed or denied,
I am *ordering* you to. Because a significant part of our
state funding is based on attendance. If you are not in
attendance *and* the asteroid misses us, we will face serious
financial hardships, which could result in deep cuts in
next year's athletic programs."

Yet another uneasy quiet settled over the auditorium. People stole quizzical glances at each other, all wondering the
same thing: Could this be real?

Here we were, facing the possibility of universal
calamity, *the end of the world as we knew it,* and our principal was worried about next year's *athletic* programs?

I turned to Angie. "Got your phone?"

"Sure." She pulled a black cell phone out of her bag
and started to punch in the security code. "Who are you
calling?"

"My mother," I said.

Meanwhile, loud, dissatisfied jabbering began to riffle
through the crowd. Down in the front, Alice raised her
hand again.

"Now what, Alice?" Wild Bill snapped from the stage,
making little effort to hide his annoyance.

"Excuse me for asking this, Mr. Dixon," Alice said politely, "but are you serious?"

"If this asteroid misses us, life will very quickly return to normal," Wild Bill replied.

"Not *my* life," Alice announced, and began to work her way out of her row.

"Don't go," Wild Bill said.

But Alice was going. She got to the aisle and started to march toward the back.

Some people clapped. A few slid out of their rows and followed her.

I dialed my mom's work number and got a busy signal.

Alice and her small band of followers pushed through the doors at the back of the auditorium.

The doors swung shut.

They were gone.

"Now I've seen everything," Angie whispered.

"Ahem." Up on the stage, Wild Bill Dixon cleared his throat. "Given the obvious distractions, I have asked your teachers to go light on homework and postpone any tests. Please proceed to your first-period classes."

The assembly ended.

People started to leave.

Down in front Andros Bliss stood up and looked around.

Once again our eyes met and locked.

Despite the continued possibility that the world might end shortly, goose bumps ran up my arms.

Andros began to work his way out of his row.

Was he coming to me?

4

"WHERE NO LAW IS,
THERE IS NO TRANSGRESSION."

—*Romans 4:15*

"Hello, ladies." The thrilling anticipation of a visit from Andros was abruptly extinguished by the appearance of my not-quite boyfriend, Derman Bloom, sliding toward us along the seats in our row. "Or should I say, good-bye?"

"I'm going to the library." Angie started out of the row in the other direction.

Derman sidled up beside me. He pressed his lips close to my ear and whispered, *"I have to speak to you."*

Across the auditorium, Andros suddenly stopped.

I knew what he was seeing—Derman with his lips pressed close to my ear.

Andros frowned, then turned away.

I wondered if he would stay in school.

It was questionable. Given the fact that he was rarely

here even when there wasn't the threat of global calamity.

As he left the auditorium I felt my heart sink. Struggling to swim up from the depths of my disappointment, I turned my attention back to Derman—a good person, but cursed with a terrible sense of timing.

"What's up?" I asked.

Before he could tell me, someone asked, "What do we do now?" Coming up the aisle toward us was Dave Ignazzi, Ray Neely, and Chase Hammond.

It was Ray who'd posed the question.

"Try to meet some girls, fast," Dave answered.

"Can't you think of anything else?" Chase asked as they passed us.

"No," Dave replied. "Can you?"

Derman and I shared a look.

It was a reasonable question.

We didn't *have* to go to class.

We didn't even *have* to stay in school.

On the other hand, if the asteroid missed...

Wait a minute! *What asteroid?* I still didn't know if any of this was real.

"Want to go someplace?" Derman asked hopefully, no doubt hoping to follow Dave Ignazzi's lead.

"Why don't we just stay here?" I slid back down into my cushioned auditorium chair.

My platonic boyfriend glanced around with a forlorn look on his face. The auditorium was hardly the place to be intimate.

Which suited me just fine.

He slouched in the chair beside me and pressed his

knees against the back of the seat in front of him. We had physics next, but frankly there was no rush. I pressed the redial button on Angie's phone.

"Who are you calling?" Derman asked.

"My mother," I answered. "I have to find out if this is real."

"Believe me, it's real," Derman confirmed.

The line was still busy. "How do you know?" I asked him.

"I know," he said with frightening assurance.

I studied Derman's face. As I said before, I liked him. He was sweet, and very, very smart.

I'd just never been able to find him physically attractive.

He had a thin, wispy, dark mustache. It was a baby mustache that needed to grow.

He also had terrible posture, as if at the tender age of seventeen he was already bent by the weight of the world.

The combination of the mustache and the bad posture created the unsettling illusion that Derman was older than his years. It almost made it *too* easy to imagine him as an old man.

The mustache would be a little thicker.

The shoulders would be a little more stooped.

You could picture him as a professor of philosophy trudging across a college campus with a brimming briefcase and a heavy load of texts under his arm.

Or as a pasty-faced computer programmer, hunched before the pale blue light of his computer screen.

The handsome image of Andros flitted teasingly through my consciousness. You could *not* picture Derman on a motorcycle.

"Swear you'll keep this a secret?" Derman asked.

I nodded.

He took a deep breath and let it out slowly. "I know this is going to sound completely insane, Legs..." he began, then paused.

"But," I said, just to let him know he had my fullest attention.

"I have a funny feeling it's all my fault."

"*What* is all your fault?" I asked, not comprehending.

"The asteroid."

If you're like me, you're probably tired of hearing grown-ups say that the teenaged years are a time of extreme egocentricity.

That teenagers are incredibly self-centered.

That we only think about ourselves and that we actually believe the world circles around us.

It's probably true.

But who wants to hear it all the time?

"Are you saying that *you* are responsible for this giant asteroid that may smash us all to bits?" I repeated to Derman for the sake of clarity.

"Yes."

"How?" I asked.

"I imagined it," he said.

"You...Why?"

"The Chinese test."

"You imagined an asteroid destroying the earth because of the Chinese test?" I asked, still not comprehending.

"You know I hate Chinese," Derman confessed. "I can't

believe my parents are making me take it. 'The language of the future,' they keep saying. It's so stupid. I'll never go to China. I'm terrified of airplanes. All the waiters in Chinese restaurants speak English. What's the point?"

"I think we're getting off the track," I said. It was something Derman was prone to do. "Let's get back to the asteroid."

Derman yawned. It seemed as if everyone in school except me had had a sleepless night. "Oh, yeah, so instead of studying for the test last night, I read some dumb article about asteroids." He paused again. "Jeez, did you hear that, Legs? Some dumb article.... It even *sounds* like Chinese. Like sum dum chicken. Or sum dum rice with bean sprouts." He winced. "They make me eat bean sprouts. God, I can't believe I was born into a family of vegetarians..."

"Focus, Derman."

"Right. So the article speculated on the possibility of an asteroid hitting the earth, and what would happen if it did. I mean, total cataclysm. Nuclear winter. Six-hundred-foot tidal waves. Earthquakes. Entire cities leveled. And I just got totally into it. Like, imagining what it would be like. Visualizing it. Think of it, Legs. No more Chinese. No more bean sprouts. No more tofu. No more parents. No more school."

"No more life," I reminded him.

"Well, yeah, I didn't think it through completely," he admitted. "But I did it, Legs. I imagined this huge asteroid smashing the earth to bits. I mean, I *seriously* fantasized about it. I pretty much got to the point where I believed it was going to happen."

"Just because you didn't want to take the Chinese test?" I asked. "Isn't that a little *extreme*?"

Derman yawned. "In retrospect, yes."

"So, just out of curiosity," I said. "When exactly did you imagine this?"

"Just before nine o'clock."

"Which is when it appeared on the Internet," I said.

Derman stared off into space. "Exactly."

Sum dum articles affect us in strange ways.

For instance, I'd read that biologists at the Togiak National Wildlife Refuge near Anchorage, Alaska, had noticed that some non-mating walruses were climbing to the top of a high cliff and jumping off.

They were part of a herd of more than twelve thousand.

The walruses, each of which weighed around two thousand pounds, tended to splat when they landed on the rocks below.

In other words, it was sort of a lover's leap for walruses.

The biologists were upset. They wanted to know why the walruses were doing this.

It was obvious to me.

They were non-mating.

Which just goes to show you. Scientists don't understand anything about love.

The truth was, I understood very little about love.

Except that I'd never experienced it.

And time might be running out.

"WHAT DO YOU CALL A FORTUNE-TELLING DWARF
WHO'S ON THE RUN FROM THE LAW?

A SMALL MEDIUM AT LARGE."

—*Derman Bloom*

Was the asteroid real?

Was the government covering it up to prevent mass
hysteria and panic?

Life is filled with unanswered questions.

In 1955 Albert Einstein's ophthalmologist reportedly
attended the great scientist's autopsy and removed Mr.
Einstein's eyes. He allegedly placed them in a jar filled
with formaldehyde and kept the jar in a safe-deposit box
for nearly forty years. In 1993 he offered them to any
interested buyers for the price of $5 million.

Were there any takers?

In 1995 a woman in England drilled a hole into her
skull to test the theory that a human being's brain functions better if the blood is allowed to circulate to the
topmost part.

Was she right?

(Just between you and me, I can't imagine that her brain functioned any *worse.)*

Here's another mystery.

Mr. Dante, my physics teacher, was completely bald. Part of this was clearly due to genetics. The rest he chose to shave away, thus giving his head the shiny appearance of a well-oiled globe.

To make up for his lack of head hair, Mr. Dante wore a salt and pepper beard, which started at mid-ear and descended around his chin. It was an odd sight. Bald on top, hairish on the bottom.

So how was it possible for there to be dandruff on the lapels of the blue blazer he wore every day?

I was thinking about this because Derman and I had left the auditorium and were now in physics class.

"Should this asteroid actually impact the earth," Mr. Dante was saying, "it will most certainly be remembered as one of the most momentous events in the history of man."

I raised my hand. "Will be remembered by whom?"

Mr. Dante paused and scratched his beard. The lines between his eyes deepened. "You mean, because the human race will be annihilated and there won't be anyone left to do the remembering?"

"Uh-huh."

"Good point, Allegra," said our physics teacher. "However, let's look at it from a historical perspective. Scientists now believe that just such an event as this occurred roughly sixty-five million years ago. Does anyone know what the result of that cataclysmic impact was?"

No one raised their hand to answer. Possibly because there was hardly anyone in the class. Only five seats were occupied. The rest had been left empty by people who had, or thought they had, something better to do.

I guess not everyone cared as much about next year's athletic programs as Mr. Dixon.

Still, it was the sort of situation that makes you wonder why *you* don't have anything better to do.

Were the five of us who chose to remain in school just complete and total losers?

On the other hand, how many of those who had left really did have something better to do?

How many were just pretending they did?

And didn't that somehow make those of us who stayed in school winners?

After all, weren't we the ones with enough self-assurance *not* to follow the crowd? Or were we merely five suck-ups betting the asteroid would miss?

Isn't it amazing how you can take almost any situation and twist it around to make it look different?

But then again, what *is* reality?

Take Andros Bliss, for instance.

Was he for real?

Was he a winner?

I thought so.

And yet, it was extremely unlikely that he was still in school. (I'd looked for him in the hall after Derman and I left the auditorium to come to physics.)

Meanwhile, no one had risen to Mr. Dante's bait regarding that cataclysmic event that occurred roughly sixty-five million years ago.

"Well," Mr. Dante said, "it caused the extinction of the dinosaurs."

Mr. Dante liked the dramatic pause and used it frequently. He used it here. No one reacted.

He frowned. "Don't you see?"

Dee Vine raised her hand. "Are you saying that an asteroid squashed all the dinosaurs?"

"No, no," replied our physics teacher. "The asteroid itself probably measured less than five miles. But it hit the earth at something like fifty thousand miles an hour, creating an impact equal to the force of a million nuclear weapons."

Another dramatic pause.

I regret to report that the few of us still in attendance seemed to care.

We sat there like so many lumps in a bowl of oatmeal.

It's hard to focus when you're wondering if this day may be your last.

"Don't you see?" our physics teacher asked. "The event equal to a million nuclear weapons wreaked utter havoc. The shock created a wave of ocean water so huge that it literally washed away low-lying parts of continents. It caused earthquakes everywhere. It threw so much dirt and dust into the air that it blotted out the sun and caused a perpetually frigid winter night for decades, destroying all plant life, and leading to the starvation and obliteration of nine-tenths of the earth's animals."

"Is that what's going to happen to us?" Dee asked uneasily.

"It could," Mr. Dante replied.

"Oh, great," someone else groaned.

"In a way, it is," Mr. Dante went on. "It's extraordinary. Don't you see? If it weren't for the last asteroid, we humans probably never would have evolved. There's almost an eerie sense of poetry to it."

Here we were on the eve of destruction and my physics teacher was talking about an eerie sense of poetry?

It was then that I lost interest in Mr. Dante's dandruff.

And in his discussion of the coming cataclysm.

Maybe it was because all that talk about the end of life reminded me of the single most painful fact of my existence: That I had no life.

I assume by now you've noticed.

My conscious hours were divided into segments spent attending to other people's needs.

To fill the empty moments in between, I studied, read, watched, and absorbed every obscure and unimportant bit of information that crossed my path.

I was slim, but I suffered from informational obesity.

To fill the hollowness of my being, I had become a human data bank of useless and irrelevant information.

But one huge glowing fact rose above all others, shining like the star atop the Christmas tree of life: If the end came the next morning, I would die alone.

Having never experienced love.

Or passion.

Or Bliss.

It seemed like the right moment to stand up.

"Yes, Allegra?" said Mr. Dante.

"I'm sorry," I said, "but I really don't think I can take any more of this."

Mr. Dante's eyebrows rose. "Oh?"

"I've come to school my whole life to learn," I went on. "To find answers to questions. But I see now that school can't answer the ultimate question."

"Which is?" Mr. Dante asked.

"Will we live or die?"

Mr. Dante turned to the rest of the class. "Does anyone else feel that way?"

The few heads left bobbed up and down.

"Don't forget, there's only a 50 percent chance of obliteration," Mr. Dante tried to remind us.

"It's too late," I said. "We're all thoroughly depressed."

I started toward the door.

"Wait, Legs." Derman rose from his seat and faced our teacher. "Mr. Dante, in honor of the possible end of the world as we know it, I've decided to tell everyone exactly what I think of them. In your case, I'd like you to know that I sort of respect you as a teacher, and your classes are pretty interesting."

Mr. Dante blinked with surprise, then allowed a small smug smile to appear on his lips. "Why, thank you, Derman."

"I'm not finished," Derman continued. "Here's what I don't like. I don't like the way you always say, 'Don't you see?' It's demeaning and it makes us feel stupid. The only way we could always know what you're leading up to would be if we were mind readers. But we're not. And neither are you."

And now it was Derman who paused dramatically. "So, if we all live through this, I hope you won't say it anymore. And if we don't live through it, well, that's life."

* ★ *

I waited for Derman out in the hall.

"That was wonderful," I said proudly.

"You really liked it?" he asked.

"Loved it," I said.

Derman gave me a searching look. "Then maybe it's time I told *you* the truth."

I instantly regretted my enthusiasm.

"Now isn't a good time," I said.

"There are no more good times," he replied. "Allegra, I love you. I've always loved you. No matter what I've done to the contrary, the existence of my love remains a single constant."

"What do you mean, 'no matter what I've done to the contrary?'" I asked. "What have you done?"

Derman stared at the floor.

"Derman?" I was puzzled.

He looked back up at me with puppy-dog eyes. "Why didn't you answer your phone last night?"

Talk about coming straight out of left field.

"What are you talking about?" I asked. "I was studying for the Chinese test. What does that have to do with anything?"

Derman sighed. "Everything."

The human brain is 74 percent water. Sometimes that water gets pretty murky.

Consider this: A few years ago a man in Fort Worth, Texas, robbed a bank. The police were waiting outside to arrest him when he left. How did they know he was going to rob the bank?

He'd stood on line wearing a ski mask.

I was standing outside physics with Derman, feeling like I was wearing a ski mask in a tank of murky water, when down at the end of the hall someone passed, then stepped back and looked at us.

It was Andros. So he *was* still in school!

My heart skipped a beat and did a triple jump.

"Who's that?" Derman asked.

"No one," I said.

"Why's he looking at you like that?" Derman demanded.

"I don't know," I replied dreamily.

"Why are *you* looking at *him* like that?"

"I don't know."

"Oh, wonderful," Derman groaned miserably. "Here I am professing my eternal undying love to you, and meanwhile, you're in love with someone else."

That snapped me out of my daze.

"I'm not in love with him," I said. "I don't even know him."

"You *wish* you did," Derman said spitefully.

"No." I shook my head.

Derman rolled his disbelieving eyes toward the ceiling. "Don't let me stand in your way, Legs. There may not be much time left. At least one of us might as well die feeling fulfilled."

He almost brought tears to my eyes. Who would have thought he could be so gallant?

"Oh, Derman." I placed my hand on his shoulder and

gazed wistfully into his beady brown eyes. "In another time, or another place, maybe it would have been different."

"And maybe you're just full of pig poop," he replied bitterly. "Now, go, sweet princess, seek your prince."

I looked down the hall again, but Andros had vanished.

"He can't have gone far," Derman said. "What are you waiting for?"

It was a good question. One I couldn't answer.

Perhaps I was afraid.

Of what Andros might turn out to be.

Of what I might turn out to be.

Anyway, I chickened out. It seemed like a reasonable time to change the subject.

"What about the asteroid?" I asked.

"What about it?" Derman replied.

"Do you still think you caused it?"

Derman's eyes took on a slightly blank, unfocused appearance. As if he'd shifted his vision inward.

"I...don't know," he answered. "I mean, doesn't it seem just too incredibly coincidental *not* to have some cause and effect relationship? The chances of an event like this happening are probably ten trillion to one, and yet on the very night I wished for it—not less than five minutes *after* I wished for it—it seems to be coming true."

What a relief!

We were back in the abstract.

"I guess part of what's bothering me is this," Derman went on. "If God is truly all-seeing and all-knowing, why is he so selective about which prayers he chooses to act on? I mean, I've fantasized about a lot of things and never got them. On the other hand, what about the terrible things that happen that you can't imagine anyone fantasizing about? Like cancer and Barney the dinosaur?"

I had no answer.

Maybe there was no answer. I put my hand in my pocket and realized I still had Angie's cell phone.

"Let's go to the library," I said.

"Why?" asked Derman.

"Isn't that where we always go for answers?"

A company in St. Louis, Missouri, makes artificial dead-body scents to help train dogs to find corpses.

One is called Pseudo Burned Victim.

Another is called Pseudo Drowned Victim (can dogs smell underwater?).

There is also Pseudo Corpse One for bodies less than thirty days old, and Pseudo Corpse Two for bodies more than thirty days old.

What will the world smell like if the asteroid hits?

I was surprised by the amount of activity in the library, where groups of students were gathered around each of the six computers with Internet access.

I was further surprised to find Alice Hackett at one of

the computers, surrounded by a bunch of guys, mostly asocial brainiacs, all staring over her shoulder at the screen.

"I thought you left school," I said.

From the middle of her crowd of boys, Alice looked up
at me. "Why would I do that?"

"Because you refused to stay so that we'd get state
money for our athletic programs."

"I was simply making a statement, Legs," Alice replied.
"We have to stay informed. Information is ammunition.
Did you know that only seven teachers are still here?
Makes you wonder who hates school more, the teachers or
the students?"

"Is that ammunition or information?" I asked.

Alice pointed at the computer screen. "This is the most
recent shot of the asteroid. Take a look."

Derman and I squeezed in among the asocial brainiacs
and looked over Alice's shoulder at the computer. The
image on the screen was of starry space. I didn't see anything that resembled a killer asteroid.

Alice pressed her finger against the screen. "It's right
about there, I think."

"Where?" I asked.

"You can't see it," she explained. "It's non-radiative.
They know it's there because as it moves it blocks out the
light of known stars."

"If it's there at all," I said.

In a rush, the brainiacs all turned irate on me.

"Don't tell me you're still buying into that government
crap," one of them snorted.

"Come on, Legs, you've got the intelligence to know
better," said another.

Did I? I still wasn't certain. One thing was for sure, however—I definitely didn't like the idea of not being able to see the asteroid. It made it a silent, invisible killer.

All the more ominous.

"The 1989 asteroid missed us by only six hours," Alice said. "Scientists weren't even aware of it until after it had passed. The only reason they know about this one is that it's so much bigger. They've named it Eros."

"Eros?" Derman repeated. "Wasn't he the Greek god of love?"

"I'm sure they didn't know it might hit the earth when they named it," I pointed out.

"It is sort of ironic," Alice agreed. "I mean, the notion of being destroyed by love. Don't you think?"

"Only you artsy-fartsy types would think of that," Derman sniggered.

He and Alice did not care for each other.

"I'd rather be an artsy-fartsy type than a capitalist dork," Alice shot back at him.

Derman glowered at her. "Know what you're going to call a capitalist dork ten years from now?"

"What?"

"Boss," Derman announced with an air of superiority.

Alice smiled sardonically. "Not if Eros hits."

I monitored this intellectual jousting contest with only half an ear. Most of my attention was drawn outside, through a library window to the parking lot.

Where Andros was astride his dented red motorcycle, pulling on his helmet.

He kicked down.

A small cloud of whitish smoke burst out of the tailpipe.

Andros started away, out of the parking lot.

And vanished.

"Legs?" Derman tugged at my arm and we moved on to the next computer, where another group was logged into a data stream continually updating the speed of the asteroid Eros, its estimated time of arrival, and projected point of impact.

It was now expected to strike the Pacific Ocean somewhere near the Marshall Islands.

"Where's all this data coming from?" I asked.

"Amateur astronomers all over the world," a brainiac answered, and pointed at his screen. "Check this out. Impact probability just dropped to 46 percent."

"That's good news, isn't it?" I asked.

"Negligible," the boy replied without taking his eyes off the screen. "Large asteroids have unpredictable and irregular paths. Impact probability could be 46 percent now and 96 percent in fifteen minutes."

"We're also looking at a margin of error of plus or minus 7 percent," added another. "Which means that a 46 percent impact probability could actually be as high as 53 percent."

"Is it my imagination or are you guys almost rooting for this thing to hit us?" I asked.

The boys took their eyes off the computer screen and gave each other quizzical looks.

"No way," said one of them.

"It's just interesting," a second chimed in.

"Although, it would be pretty awesome," admitted a third.

Derman and I moved onto the next computer, where Ray Neely and Chase Hammond sat with Dave Ignazzi, who was patched into a chat room with a bunch of girls from Tucson, Arizona.

"You guys are *not* for real," Derman moaned in disbelief.

"Chill out," Dave said. "I think this girl likes me."

"He told her he's six foot two and the captain of the football team," Ray explained.

"She's in *Arizona,* for Pete's sake!" Derman reminded him.

"Hey, if she were any closer, he probably wouldn't stand a chance," said Chase.

"The world may be coming to an end and you're flirting with girls you'll never meet?" I asked.

"Can you think of anything better to do?" Dave asked for the second time that day.

It made me think of Andros.

Where was he headed?

To the arms of some waiting lover?

To spend the final moments of his life in a passionate embrace?

To patch into the eternal data stream of love?

We left Dave and turned the corner where we came upon Angie sitting alone at the next computer, staring intently at the screen.

She wasn't yet aware of us.

Derman suddenly hesitated and pressed his finger to his lips.

I mouthed the words, "What's wrong?"

"I just remembered something," he whispered, backing away. "See you later." He headed out of the library.

As I watched him leave, it occurred to me that he was acting irrationally.

Then again, with the balance of our lives possibly reduced to hours, what was the point of being rational?

7

"THE MORE THREATENING...REALITY APPEARS,
THE MORE FIRMLY AND DESPERATELY
MUST WE BELIEVE."

—*Pierre Teilhard de Chardin*

I forgot to mention that besides being beautiful, sexy, and smart, Angie is also rich. And yet, strange as it may seem, she, like I, had never had a serious boyfriend.

The best way I can explain this is with the following joke: A man is shipwrecked on an island with a beautiful, sexy, incredibly famous movie star. Let's call her Venus. The man and Venus fall in love and the relationship becomes physical.

The man can't believe his good fortune. To be stuck on an island being physical with the incomparable Venus is every man's dream!

Things go well for a few months, but then something begins to gnaw at the man. Soon it's driving him crazy.

Finally one day he asks Venus if she really loves him.

She says she does.

Would she do anything for him? he asks.

Yes, she replies.

Would she wear men's clothes?

Okay, she says.

And a hat? he asks.

Okay, she says.

And could he draw a mustache on her upper lip?

Uh, if you insist, she replies, starting to wonder.

And finally, would she mind if he called her Joe?

Okay, she says.

So Venus gets dressed up like a man named Joe with a mustache and a hat.

Now what? she asks.

Let's take a walk down the beach, the man says.

They walk down the beach.

Then the man stops and turns to her.

"Joe," he says in a low voice. "Can you keep a secret?"

"Sure," replies Venus, pretending to be Joe.

The man looks around to make sure no one can hear him. Then he moves close to "Joe" and whispers, "Listen, Joe, you know that incredibly beautiful, sexy movie star named Venus?"

"Yes?"

"Well, guess who's been sleeping with her?"

Angie can't have a relationship with a guy because no guy can have a relationship with her without immediately blabbing about it to the whole school.

Angie can't even tell whether a guy really likes her or is just trying to impress his friends by being with her.

In the library I looked over her shoulder at her computer. The normally gray screen background was pink. In the foreground were deep red letters:

THE RULES OF VIRGINITY
1. VIRGINITY IS *NOT* A STATE OF MIND
2. ONCE IT'S GONE, IT'S GONE FOR GOOD
3. THE ABOVE NOT WITHSTANDING, EVERYONE DESERVES A SECOND CHANCE

"What's that?" I asked.

With the look of a doe startled by headlights, Angie spun around in her chair. "Legs! What are you doing here?"

"I originally came to give back your cell phone," I answered. "But now I'm reading over your shoulder. Why are you on the virginity page?"

"Oh, uh, I was just surfing around." Angie quickly jumped back a few cyber pages and pointed at some information, which now flashed on the screen. "Did you know that the average human body produces 350 feet of hair in a lifetime?"

"Not in our lifetimes if Eros hits," I said.

Angie scrolled to some more information and read: "The average fingernail grows an inch and a half a year. Each square inch of human skin contains twenty feet of blood vessels, seventy-two feet of nerves, and fifty thousand nerve endings."

I reached over her shoulder and fiddled with the mouse, scrolling screens back to:

THE RULES OF VIRGINITY

"What about this?" I asked.

"It's nothing," Angie said. "I was just wondering."

"About virginity?"

"It's not important," Angie said uneasily. "Well, it *is* important. But maybe not anymore."

"Oh, well, I'm glad you've cleared it up for me," I quipped.

Angie gave me a helpless look. "I'm not making much sense, am I?"

"No, but under the circumstances, I'm not sure it makes a lot of difference."

I suppose it takes the threat of global calamity to make us aware of how much we are governed by rules.

Our lives are filled with them.

From the moment we wake up in the morning we follow the rules.

We wash.

We dress.

We don't kill the first person we see.

We go to school.

We attend classes (usually).

We sit.

We listen.

And yet, the very rules we learn are often at odds with each other.

For instance, we learn in English that the letter *i* comes before *e* except after *c*.

And what immediately breaks that rule?

Science.

"What's this?" It was Dave Ignazzi, joining me behind Angie.

"None of your business," Angie snapped irritably.

"THE RULES OF VIRGINITY," Dave read.

"Get lost, Dave," Angie warned him.

"If ever there was a rule meant to be broken," Ray Neely mumbled.

"What happened to the girls from Arizona?" I asked.

"Dave asked if they were wearing underwear," Ray reported dismally. "So they put him on bozo filter and started talking to some other guys."

"Not surprising," I said.

"Hey, it was an honest question," Dave said defensively.

"For someone with the intellectual depth of a speed bump," Angie mumbled.

"Hey, Angie, you want to break the rules of virginity with me?" Dave asked with a leer.

"Drop dead." Angie turned off the computer. "Come on, Legs, let's get out of here."

I suspect that the bozo filter is one of those things, like soda pop, tennis sneakers, and hero sandwiches, that goes by different names in different regions.

For us, it is that ingenious device on a computer that filters out annoying people in a cyber chat room.

You put them on bozo filter and they simply disappear from your screen.

Could you imagine having one in real life?

Putting your annoying little sister on bozo filter?

So that you could neither hear nor see her?

Oddly, I felt no need to put my parents on one.

Most of the time it felt as if they were on one already.

Besides, if I put them on bozo filter, they couldn't fulfill their primary purpose in my life—that of being my very own personal living, breathing ATM machines.

"Where are we going?" I asked Angie as we left the library. I was holding the cell phone, trying my mom's work again.

"To find Derman," Angie said.

"Funny you should mention that," I said as I dialed. "He was just here. Then he saw you and suddenly had to leave."

"Figures. He's such a chicken."

"Why?" I asked. Once again I got a busy signal.

"Because he is," she said.

"Then why do you want to find him?" I handed the phone back to her.

"So that we can all live or die in peace."

Some random facts about life, death, and pain:

1. A female pigeon cannot lay an egg unless it sees another pigeon, or itself in a mirror.
2. Mosquitoes have killed more people than all the world's wars combined.
3. If a human baby grew as fast as a baby blue whale, it would be sixty-five feet tall by the age of two.
4. In the Middle Ages more than nine million people in Europe

were condemned as witches and burned at the stake.
5. In 1859, twenty-four rabbits were released in Australia. Six
   years later the rabbit population there was approximately two
   million.
6. Tiger shark embryos fight to the death while still in the
   mother's womb. Only the survivor is born.
7. Pain travels through the body at a speed of 350 feet per
   second.

"Why do I have the feeling that I'm being kept in the dark?" I asked as we walked down the deserted hallway.

"Because you are," Angie confirmed.

"Then why won't you tell me what's going on?" I asked.

"I will," Angie replied. "But not quite yet."

"Why not?"

"Because...I'm not sure myself."

"This does not sound like you," I observed.

Angie stopped in the middle of the hall.

She let out a long sigh as if signaling that she'd arrived at a decision. "Remember the three rules of virginity?"

"It's not a state of mind," I recited. "Once it's gone, it's gone forever. But everyone deserves a second chance."

"I need to know what you think, Legs."

"About the rules?"

She nodded.

"I think...the first two are pretty obvious," I said. "The third one is questionable."

Angie winced. "Because we're talking about a physical act?"

"Basically."

"But what if you were uncertain about the physical act itself?" she asked. "About whether it had actually occurred."

"Well...then I suppose that it's up to you," I said. "I mean, you can argue that we each create our own reality. We can believe whatever we choose to believe."

"I agree, Legs," Angie said. "But it's not that simple."

"Why not?" I asked.

"Because virginity isn't...an issue you face alone." Her voice cracked. "At least, not when...its status is called into question."

Angie's eyes began to glisten.

Something about the anguish in her voice caused my brain to skid to a stop.

My closest friend wiped a tear from her eye.

"OhmyGod!" I gasped.

I pulled her close and hugged her, hating myself for being so incredibly thick and oblivious.

"I'm so stupid," I cried guiltily. "I didn't know. I wasn't thinking. I've been totally insensitive."

Angie sniffed and trembled. "It's okay, Legs. I didn't make it obvious. Besides, the world may be ending. That kind of thing can be distracting."

This was true, but it didn't make me feel any better. I brushed a lock of reddish-brown hair out of her eyes—a feeble attempt at a soothing, reassuring caress.

"You want to talk about it?" I asked.

"Not yet. I have to think. I mean, I just don't want to be alone."

I looked up and down the hallway.

It was empty.

We were alone.

I had the feeling that except for the library, the building was deserted.

So much for next year's athletic programs.

I looked back at my dear, dear friend, her head bent, her shoulders stooped, her entire being so obviously racked with misery.

"There's just one thing I *have* to ask," I said in a low voice. "Were you forced?"

Angie instantly straightened up, her reddened eyes wide with surprise. "No! Nothing like that. I mean, like I said before, I'm not even sure it happened."

"Then why are you so upset?" I asked.

"Well..." Angie sniffed. *"Something* happened."

8

"IF THE POLICE ARREST A MIME, DO THEY HAVE TO
INFORM HIM OF HIS RIGHT TO REMAIN SILENT?"

—*Chase Hammond*

The angler fish lives in absolute darkness miles beneath
the surface of the ocean. It is called an angler because of
the long threads of flesh that grow from around its mouth
and head. At the ends of these threads are little flesh
lights that attract other fish. When another fish gets close
enough, the angler eats it.

When scientists first discovered the angler fish, they
noticed that a smaller parasitic fish was often attached to
it. They subsequently found that the parasite was actually
a male angler fish, and that the larger host was always a
female.

In fact, it was revealed that the little male literally
fused with the bigger female and spent its entire life living
off its mate.

In some respects, I can understand why this has to happen.

The deep sea is so huge and dark, that once you find someone you really like, you want to hold on.

But it seems to me that a female could just as easily attach itself to a male for a free ride through life.

And yet, it's always the female that must bear the burden.

Somehow, I'm not surprised.

Angie and I got into my car and left school. She wanted to find Derman. I wanted to find anyone who could officially confirm or deny the asteroid.

"A lot of people are saying this is Armageddon," Angie said, dabbing her eyes as I drove.

"Ah, yes," I replied. "The final battle between the forces of good and evil."

"I don't really see how it fits," she said. "I mean, if the asteroid hits us and we all die, isn't that evil?"

"I think it may depend on how you look at it," I said. "There are a lot of people who think that *we* are evil. So for them the asteroid destroying us would be good."

"So they think if the asteroid misses us, evil wins?" Angie asked.

"I guess," I said.

"Doesn't it sound a little bit *off* to you?"

It did.

A station wagon pulled alongside us. The back was loaded with suitcases, cardboard boxes and duffle bags. On the roof was a canoe and two large Styrofoam coolers.

A grim-looking man sat behind the wheel. Next to him sat his grim-looking wife. In the seat behind them were three sullen-looking children.

"Where do they think they're going?" Angie wondered aloud.

"Away?" I guessed.

We stopped at an intersection. The light was red. The traffic passed. Then came the low rumble of a motorcycle engine.

Andros Bliss rode through the intersection, steering his motorcycle with his right hand.

Tucked under his left arm was a bright yellow and green surfboard with a black stripe down the middle.

"It's him," Angie said.

"I know," I answered, not quite believing what I was seeing.

"Where do you think *he's* going?" she asked.

"Given the fact that he's carrying a surfboard, my vote would be for the beach."

"In the middle of February?" Angie asked.

"Let's see." I made a quick right.

A moment later we were behind Andros.

So close that the scent of his exhaust seeped in through the car windows.

"What are you doing?" Angie sounded absolutely incredulous.

"Following him, obviously." My heart had begun to beat fast. Everything was tingling. I could scarcely remember ever doing anything so impetuous. With such total disregard for common sense or logic that it almost felt criminal.

"Why?" Angie asked.

"Why not?" I countered gleefully. Everything was in extra sharp focus, my entire being abuzz with unexpected excitement.

I felt so alive!

BLURP! The single sudden blaring burst of a siren startled us.

Angie twisted around in her seat. "Uh, Legs?"

"That's me."

"I think you better pull over."

My eyes went to the rearview mirror.

Blue and red lights were flashing behind me.

Of course.

I pulled to the side of the road and watched Andros Bliss, his red motorcycle, and yellow and green surfboard disappear into the traffic ahead.

The police car sat behind us, lights flashing.

"Why did he pull us over?" Angie asked.

"I don't have a clue," I said.

And yet it seemed perfectly justifiable.

I felt as if I'd broken a law.

The law of reason.

There was no logical reason for me to suddenly follow Andros.

And this officer, no doubt a member of the Reason Police, was foiling my one single attempt at being spontaneous.

At not making sense.

For the second time that day, someone tapped a ring on my window. Only this time it was a gold wedding band.

I looked up through the shatterproof glass into the

inscrutable face of an officer of the law, then opened the door a little. "Sorry, my window doesn't work."

"License and registration, please."

I found both and handed them over.

He took them without a word and went back to his car.

The city of Los Angeles has many freeways. I've read that at any given moment, nearly one quarter of the city is covered by vehicles. People there sometimes do strange things in their cars. The following is a list of activities that resulted in drivers being pulled over by the LAPD:

Eating a can of chili.

Cutting a child's hair.

Brushing teeth and rinsing with a cup of water (out the window, I hope).

Typing on a laptop computer.

Changing a baby's diaper.

Using a curling iron (think rearview mirror).

Reading a book.

Removing pantyhose (don't try this at home, kids).

Where on that list does it state that one can be pulled over for behaving unreasonably?

"Do you know why I stopped you?" the police officer asked, handing back my driver's license and registration.

I shook my head mutely.

"You made an illegal right turn on red back there."

"Really?" I swiveled around and looked back at the intersection.

"No turns on red during school days between the hours of 7:00 A.M. and 4:30 P.M.," said the officer.

The absurdity of it danced into my consciousness. "Well, I know I'm wrong and I'm not trying to weasel out of this, officer. But you have to admit that it's not exactly a school day. I mean, there's hardly anyone left at school."

"I'm not surprised," said the police officer. "Nearly a fifth of the force didn't show up for the morning shift. Makes you wonder, doesn't it?"

He was asking *me?*

"So what do you hear?" I asked back.

He responded with an offhand shrug. "My wife called a little while ago and said the president went on TV with a bunch of scientists from NASA. They're all claiming it's bull. But my uncle was a detective down in Dallas in '63 when Kennedy was shot and to this day he'll tell you Oswald didn't act alone. And you're probably too young to know about the Bay of Pigs."

"You're right," I said.

"You can't trust the government," he said. "I mean, who the hell really knows?"

"But I also think you're doing the right thing," I said with complete earnestness. "Someone has to enforce the laws. I was wrong to make that turn. It was a reckless, impetuous thing to do, but there was this guy on a motor-cycle—"

"The one with a surfboard?"

I felt my face grow hot with a blush.

The police officer smiled knowingly. "Hey, it's a beautiful day for February and the surf's up. I used to do the same thing."

I was tempted to ask if he'd ever worn a skull ring.

"So listen," he said, "I'm not going to give you a ticket,

but you better get that window fixed. And no more illegal right turns, okay?"

"I promise," I said.

"Okay, you can go. Have a nice day." He went back to his car.

Even though it may be our last! I thought.

I started my car and pulled back onto the road.

"No ticket," Angie said. "You're amazing."

"Not really," I said.

"Why not?"

"I guess he figures there's a 50 percent chance I won't be around to pay it."

The truth: I was relieved when the Reason Police pulled me over.

It made no sense to follow Andros to the beach.

I would have been pursuing a fantasy.

It scared me.

It was a journey into the unknown.

Andros and I inhabited two different universes.

I had no idea why he'd tapped on my shatterproof window that morning.

I had no idea what trading looks with him in the hallway and the auditorium meant.

What I did know was that I had my friends.

I had my safe little emotionally secure shatterproof world.

I had a nice nonthreatening boy like Derman who loved me but would never do anything about it (thank God).

I had beautiful Angie's shirttails to ride socially.

(I'm not always this brutally honest about myself. But let's face it. When you could be dead in less than twenty-four hours, what's the point of pretending?)

This would be me for the rest of my life, no matter how short or long: safe, smart, shatterproof, insulated from anything out of my control.

But without Bliss?

"TIME IS A GREAT TEACHER, BUT UNFORTUNATELY
IT KILLS ALL ITS PUPILS."

—*Berlioz*

We parked in front of Derman's house. As you may have gathered, Derman's parents were hippie vegetarian leftovers from another era. They lived in a low modern-looking house with lots of big picture windows and a tree growing up through the roof.

Derman's mother was some kind of artist. His father had started a rock and roll management company in the 1960s and sold it for a lot of money. Now he taught literature at a "noncompetitive" private school that Derman refused to attend.

"Here we are." I turned off the engine.

Angie slid down in her seat. "I can't."

"What do you mean?" I asked. "It was your idea to come here in the first place."

"I just changed my mind. Let's go before he sees us."

I looked back at the house. Derman was standing in the front door. He looked...disturbed.

"Too late," I said. "He sees us."

"He sees *you*," Angie corrected me from the floor. "I'm hiding."

"So?"

Angie yawned. "So I'll stay here and take a nap. Bye."

I got out of the car and went up the walk.

It was an odd sight.

There was Derman in the doorway.

And above and slightly behind him rose this rather large dark green pine tree.

Right through the roof of the house.

I felt as if I had to come up with some explanation for my presence. "Hi, I was just, uh..."

"I know why you're here," he said.

"You can't," I said. Out of the corner of my eye I glanced back at my car. Angie was not visible.

"It's just...mind-blowingly bizarre." In moments of stress, Derman often retreated to the language of his elders.

"It is?" I said, not comprehending at all.

"I was just thinking about you," he said.

"So?"

"I was just picturing us," he went on. "Me at the front door. You coming up the walk."

"Why?" I asked.

Derman gave me a "Don't-you-get-it?" look.

That's when I remembered the Chinese test and his asteroid fantasy.

"Oh, no, don't tell me you *willed it*," I groaned.

"How else can you explain it?" he asked.

"That you were thinking about me a second ago and now I'm here?" I said. "Try coincidence."

"A coincidence?" Derman raised a skeptical eyebrow. "Is that like visualizing a giant asteroid appearing out of nowhere and destroying the earth?"

"Give it up, Derman," I scoffed. "You can't be serious."

He raised his hands defensively. "Hey, listen, I find it pretty incredible myself. But you have to admit there's something to it. I mean, the evidence is starting to add up."

"Evidence of what?"

"That my thought processes are somehow connected to bigger things," he said.

"You think you're God?" I decided to cut to the chase.

"I said, 'connected,'" Derman stressed.

"Derman, it sounds to me like you're becoming *discon*nected. From reality, that is."

"Okay, fine." He sounded annoyed. "*You* tell me what you're doing here."

I couldn't, of course. So I went on the offensive. "No. If you're so darn prescient, why don't *you* tell *me?*"

Derman wagged his finger at me. "It doesn't work that way."

"What doesn't work that way?"

"Whatever's going on with my thoughts," he said. "I don't have any control over it. Things just happen. I can't make them happen."

"Wait a minute," I said. "I thought you just said you willed me to be here. I thought you said you willed Eros to come and bash the earth?"

Derman shook his head. "I think about things, I *imagine* things, and they happen. But if I think about *making* them happen, they don't."

I stared at him in disbelief. "You've gone totally flaky, Derman."

He shrugged. We'd reached an impasse. "Want to come in?"

"Yes, no, I don't know." I still didn't know what I was doing there.

He nodded as if he understood *that* too. "Come in, I want to show you something."

I followed him into the house, which smelled like a pine tree.

"Scientists estimate that the odds of a person being hit by a meteorite are approximately ten trillion to one," he said as we passed the living room with the tree trunk rising through the middle of it.

"So I've heard," I replied. "But in our case, it's something like 46 percent."

"As of five minutes ago 43 percent," Derman corrected me.

"That's good news, isn't it?" I asked. "I mean, allowing for the asteroid's irregular path and a margin of error of up to plus or minus 7 percent."

Derman had a glint in his eye. "Very good, Ms. Wizard. But did you know that it almost happened in 1954? A meteorite about the size of a softball smashed through a ceiling of a house in Alabama. It bounced along the floor and hit a person on the leg. There's a lot of debate over whether that constitutes actually being 'hit.'"

"You mean, because it bounced off the floor first?"

"Exactly," Derman said. "One assumes the chances of being struck by a ricochetting meteorite aren't quite as extreme as a direct hit. On the other hand, on the night of Friday, October 9, 1992, a meteor about the size of a bowling ball smashed into the right rear fender of a 1980 Chevy Malibu in Peekskill, New York."

"And?"

"The car was owned by this girl in high school. She sold the meteorite to a collector for $59,000. And she sold the car to a museum for $10,000. Guess what she paid for the car?"

"How would I know?"

"A hundred bucks. That means she made a net profit of $68,900."

"Gross profit," I corrected him. "She still had to replace the car."

"Good point. But needless to say, she came out way ahead."

We went down a hall lined with lumpy earth-tone weavings intermixed with colorful beads. Some of them had bits of tree bark, pine cones, and pine needles woven into them.

We came to Derman's room. I noticed that something was different about his bedroom door.

"You added a window," I said. The window was about a foot square and had wire running through it in a crisscrossing pattern.

"Yes." Derman pushed on the door. "My parents are into giving me my own space and privacy, you know? Letting me set my own rules and curfews. They've always had this attitude that kids are just little adults and should be treated as such. What a load of crap. So putting a security window in my door was like the most rebellious thing I could do." He paused and then pointed at the hallway floor. "Oh, and I added this."

I looked down. On the floor outside his door was a black rubber industrial-looking Welcome mat.

"I'm even thinking of papering my walls in faux cinder block," he announced brightly.

"You're really trying to make them insane," I concluded.

"Hey," Derman replied with a wry smile. "Isn't that what teenagers are *supposed* to do?"

We went into his room.

Unlike the rest of the house, the walls were bare and painted institutional light green.

A single bed was pressed against one wall.

A plain wooden chest of drawers against another.

Next to the third wall was a gray metal desk with a computer, printer, fax, and telephone.

And two gray metal office chairs on wheels.

Derman sat down at one chair facing the computer screen and gestured for me to sit in the other.

"I have a confession to make," he said, watching rows of unintelligible (to me) letters and numbers flit past on the screen. "I have become the ultimate capitalist monster. I found ways to make money off human tragedy."

"At least you're not intentionally spreading the AIDS virus," I said.

Derman yawned. "You sure know how to make a guy feel better, Legs. So look at this." He typed quickly and a new set of unintelligible figures appeared on the screen.

"These were my positions when the market opened this morning. Here's where they are now. I'm up like a 120 percent. It's unheard of."

"What does it mean?" I asked.

"Oh, that I've made about twenty-four thousand dollars today," Derman said. "Of course, it's all pretend money. But still, isn't it cool?"

"How?" I asked, not following.

Derman pointed at a waterfall of cascading symbols and numbers on one of the screens.

"Fuel oil futures," he said with a self-satisfied grin.

"I thought you invested in stocks."

"That's kid's stuff," Derman answered derisively. "The real action is in commodities futures, contracts, options, puts, calls."

Without warning he grabbed his head with his hands as if it was going to explode. "I can't believe I'm doing this! It's so sick!"

"How does it work?" I asked.

Derman wheeled back his chair and faced me. "If the asteroid hits, the sky goes dark with dust and debris."

"Nuclear winter," I said.

"Only it's not really nuclear," Derman said. "But until recently scientists thought the only way that much dust and debris could be thrown into the atmosphere was in a nuclear war."

"Right."

"So it's cold and dark," Derman went on. "People are going to need heat, gas, fuel, warm clothes, food...What else?"

What else?

Wait a minute!

The breath rushed out of my lungs in a spasm. I suddenly felt paralyzed. It seemed to take all my strength just to point a trembling finger at the computer and stammer, "Wha...what is that?"

"Just a Quotron," Derman answered, clearly mystified by my reaction. "It's no big deal. I mean, the real traders all use Bloomberg, but there's no way I could afford—"

"No, no!" I cried, still pointing my shaking finger. "What's it connected to?"

"The stock markets," Derman replied with a puzzled look. "What's wrong, Legs?"

"The *real* stock markets!?"

"Of course."

"The *real* stock markets connected to the *real* economy of this *real* country?" I asked, horrified.

"Yes," Derman answered. "What's with you?"

Instead of answering, I picked up the phone and hastily dialed my mother's office. Thank God it rang.

"Hello?"

"Oh, Mom!" I blurted. "I've been trying to get to you all day."

"Sorry, hon, it's been a little crazy here," she said in a tone conveying that it was a *normal* little crazy as opposed to an *abnormal* little crazy. "So what's up?"

"The end of the world," I said.

"Oh, yes," she chuckled. "That rumor on the Internet. Don't worry, hon, it's just a cyberhoax."

"Everyone's left school," I said.

"Sure, it's a beautiful February day," Mom replied gaily. "Midterms are over. College applications are finished. It's senior slump. Everyone's looking for an excuse."

My mother was incredibly laid back about my academics. Of course, it wasn't hard when her daughter was as compulsive about school as I was.

"The stock market's gone bonkers," I said.

"The stock market is no indication of anything except rumors, hot tips, and hunches," my mother calmly replied. "You can't take that seriously."

"You can't?" I felt like a simpleton. Was it really so obvious?

"Listen, hon, I'm entertaining a client tonight," my mother said. "I won't be home until late. If you're not up, I'll see you in the morning, okay?"

"Uh, sure."

"Love you. Bye." My mother, who was both wise and old enough to remember when flying was dangerous and sex was safe, hung up.

I put down the phone. "She says the stock market is based on rumors, hot tips, and hunches."

"Absolutely," Derman concurred cheerfully. "It's basically legalized gambling. Half these people are betting the asteroid will hit. The other half are betting it won't."

"If there even *is* an asteroid," I stressed.

"Oh, come on, Legs, get with the program already," Derman replied impatiently. "Of course there is."

Feeling light-headed, I plopped myself down on his bed. Derman sat down beside me.

"Are you okay?" He looked worried.

"I'm not sure." I pointed at the computer. "Why do you do that?"

"Play the markets?"

"Yes."

"Simple," he replied. "I was born with zero hand-eye coordination. It made me an outcast from the age of seven. I had no choice but to seek other arenas in which to excel. Hence, the world of high finance, where I can bask in the self-congratulatory glow of knowing that while other kids are playing baseball I am preparing myself to become a billionaire. Besides, I'm Derman Bloom. The guy who puts the *fun* back in dys*fun*ctional. What else am I going to do?"

He raised an eyebrow suggestively and gave me a meaningful look.

That's when I realized that I was alone with him, reclining on his bed in his bedroom.

"Derman..." Feeling apprehensive, I sat up. "You're not serious."

He leaned toward me, weaving his fingers together as if in prayer. "You don't have to be afraid, Legs. You know I'd never do anything disagreeable. I just want you to think about it."

I slid away and pressed my back against the wall. "Derman, you're sweet and cute and I'm terribly fond of you, but I can't."

"You didn't think about it," he said accusingly.

"You're right."

Derman's entire demeanor sagged. "You had to tell me I'm sweet and cute. Don't you know what that means, Legs? Cute guys are the ones girls confide in about the guys they *really* like. Sweet guys are the ones who pay for everything and don't ask for anything in return. Come on,

Legs, let me be a real guy. Just for once let me have a near-life experience!"

"Sorry, Derman."

"Even if we may all be dead tomorrow?" he argued.

"There's only a 43 percent chance. *If* the asteroid even exists."

Derman glanced over at the computer. "It's back up to 45 percent. And when you factor in the 7 percent margin of error—"

"The answer is still no."

Derman put his hands flat on his knees and shut his eyes.

"What are you doing?" I asked nervously.

"Visualizing."

I have to admit that I was curious and somewhat uneasy about the outcome.

I mean, does anyone really know?

Anything's possible.

Derman opened his eyes. "So?"

Nothing had happened.

No voice in my head had compelled me to leap into his arms.

No uncontrollable urge had swept through me.

Nothing.

Then the doorbell rang.

Derman went pale. His eyes widened fearfully.

"What's wrong?" I asked.

His mouth opened, but no words came out.

The doorbell rang again.

"Aren't you going to answer it?" I asked.

Derman's eyes darted left and right with frantic rapidity.

"What is it, Derman?" I asked.

"It's Angie," he gasped.

I knew that he was probably right. But how in the world could he...?

"How do you know that?" I asked.

"I...I thought of it," Derman stammered. "I tried to visualize you being overcome with passion for me, but, instead, this picture of Angie ringing the doorbell got stuck in my head. I couldn't get rid of it."

The doorbell rang insistently.

"Looks like you're not going to get rid of her either," I said.

Derman straightened up. He took a deep breath and puffed his chest out. "All right. It's time we all faced the music." He stood up.

"What are you talking about?" I asked.

"You better come with me," he said.

"Why?"

"Because."

We went back through the perpetually pine-scented living room.

Derman opened the door.

Angie was standing there, of course.

The three of us engaged in a round of awkward looks. It was odd, since normally Angie and Derman had between little and nothing to do with each other.

And yet I could sense from their looks that something truly unexpected was in the offing.

"Why don't we sit," Derman suggested.

Around the tree trunk in the middle of the living room was an area of sunken floor where large Indian print pillows were scattered.

The idea was to gather around the tree and lounge on the pillows while meditating greater truths, or eating ice cream.

The three of us stepped down into the sunken area and made ourselves comfortable on the pillows.

"Well, uh, here we are." Derman clapped his hands and displayed a frozen smile. He seemed extremely nervous.

Angie's eyes darted back and forth between us.

I raised my hand. "Can I make a suggestion?"

"Go ahead," answered Derman.

"Why don't we skip the preop procedures and just cut the patient open?"

Derman and Angie shared a look.

"Well, remember last night?" Derman asked. "The news of the asteroid was everywhere and your phone was off the hook."

I rolled my eyes impatiently. "I already told you I was studying Chinese."

"So I called Angie," Derman said.

"And?" I was getting more impatient.

"I just wanted someone to *talk* to," Derman said. "But Angie's parents were away—"

"Italy," Angie interjected with a dismissive shrug.

"—and she didn't want to be alone," Derman continued. "So I went over."

Just then a truly outrageous inkling plunked itself

down in the middle of my consciousness. A scenario that, when you considered Angie and Derman, was almost comical. I mean, I'm really not trying to be mean, but talk about beauty and the beast.

No, I told myself. *It's not possible.*

"You went over to talk," I said to Derman.

Neither Angie nor Derman said a word.

Instead they both yawned, and at the same time clamped their hands over their mouths.

Imagine taking a finished jigsaw puzzle and dumping it upside down on the floor.

All the pieces fall out and land in a disconnected jumble.

Now roll the tape in reverse.

The disconnected jumble flies off the floor and lands in a perfect picture.

That's what happened in my mind.

All the disconnected pieces came together into the last thing in the world I would have expected.

And not nearly as comical as I would have thought.

Turning to Derman, I felt my face grow hot with fury. "For all you knew, it was the end of the world."

He cringed. "Those first reports were totally off the wall, Legs. I mean, they weren't even talking about percent possibility of impact. It was just pure doom."

Feeling light-headed, I turned to Angie. "The three rules of virginity."

Angie bit her lip. "I don't know, Legs. I mean, I'm really not sure."

We both looked at Derman again.

His face was bright red.

"It wasn't exactly a done deal," he allowed.

"I was stupid, Legs," Angie practically pleaded. "Try to understand. I was scared. I was alone. I wasn't thinking straight."

"We really thought it was the end," added Derman.

"My best friend and my boyfriend," I sniffed.

Derman and Angie shared the guiltiest of looks.

I stood up and started toward the door.

"Where are you going?" Derman asked desperately.

"Legs, it really doesn't change anything," Angie cried.

Oh, but it did.

10

"HUMAN KIND CANNOT BEAR VERY MUCH REALITY."

—*T.S. Eliot*

Learned behaviors.

Explains why my mother cries at weddings.

And why my father shouts when he's angry.

But what do we do when we find ourselves in a situation where we don't know how to react?

Go to the movies.

Not literally, figuratively.

And so, when I learned that my "boyfriend" had betrayed me with my best friend, I stormed out.

Other movie possibilities would have been:

Grab a knife *(Slasher,* Rated R)

Let's sit down and talk this through *(My Funny Friends,* Rated PG-13)

Shave my head and join a cult *(Reality Zero,* independent film not rated)

Actually, men and women are constantly thinking of new ways to cope with betrayal.

I read about one woman who bit off a significant part of her boyfriend's tongue and flushed it down the toilet.

A Japanese woman made more than 16,000 prank calls to a man who had jilted her.

The ex-wife of an airline pilot baked him a rye bread and added marijuana to it. Just as she hoped, the pilot underwent a random drug test and was fired.

Not surprisingly, men seem to feel compelled to demonstrate their feelings of frustration in larger, more violent ways.

One man tried to shoot his wife with a bazooka. He missed but did serious damage to their home.

Another stole a four-and-one-half-ton road excavation machine and tried to demolish his girlfriend's house with it.

Oddly, as I drove away from Derman's house, I discovered that I had no desire for revenge. In fact, I realized that, in a strange way, betrayal, while devastating, can also be liberating.

It frees you of any moral obligation toward your betrayers, even though only moments before you may have thought they were the closest people in your life.

It opens up new vistas.

It may have been the middle of February.

But it felt like the perfect time to go to the beach.

✽   ✽   ✽

The day had turned sunny and warm. As I drove, the sunlight pouring in through my shatterproof windows felt soothing on the pale skin of my forearms.

Not surprisingly, traffic going to the beach was mostly nonexistent. With time to kill (oops!) before I arrived at water's edge, I let my mind go into a controlled drift.

Anywhere it wanted as long as I didn't think about those low-life canker sores, Derman and Angie.

Well, maybe just for a moment.

Just so that you know why I was angry.

I was angry at Derman because just a few hours earlier he had professed his total and undying love for me.

And even though I didn't feel the same way about him, it was still comforting to think he really felt that way. Every girl needs a guy who is madly in love with her, even if it's not reciprocated. It's important for our sense of well-being.

But why, then, would he do whatever he did with Angie?

Well, to be honest, why not?

Angie was gorgeous and sexy.

And it wasn't like he'd received any satisfaction from me.

But that was beside the point.

And I was angry at Angie because she was supposed to be my friend.

And even though she knew my relationship with Derman was only platonic, why couldn't she respect that?

I didn't know the answers to those questions.

And I wasn't going to waste a lot of time and emotional energy trying to speculate.

Not when there might be so little time left. And thus, as I drove along, I felt the oddest smile grow on my face, and an unexpected sense of pride swell in my breast.

I wasn't going to allow myself to get stuck in the past.

Instead, I was rolling, unfettered, toward the future.

Regardless of how short it might be.

I was looking ahead instead of behind.

I just hoped Andros was at the beach.

Several years ago a group of doctors got together and put forth the theory that each person has a preset level of happiness.

In other words, no matter what happens to you, you're going to be happy X amount of the time. And it won't matter how much good or bad fortune, or just plain weirdness, life hurls at you.

These doctors compared their findings to the set-point concept of weight control, which says that the brain is programmed to keep your body at a certain weight regardless of how hard you try to diet.

Boo hoo, but true.

According to the set-point theory of happiness, our well-being is basically a matter of genetics.

That means that once we're born, very little can be done to change how happy or sad we're going to be in our lives.

Researchers found that, like the song goes, money can't buy happiness. At least not any more than your genetic allocation allows.

Education doesn't seem to make a big difference. Nor

does getting married and having a family (if that's what you want).

Of course, really bad stuff, or really good stuff, was found to affect a person's mood.

But only temporarily.

Six months to a year after great tragedy or great fortune, most people are back to their set-point allotment of happiness.

I consider myself to be a basically happy person. But I am definitely the kind of person who is happier with people than without them.

Therefore, having just performed a major friendectomy (as in appendectomy), leaving me bereft of emotional support from my closest compadres, it was time to move on.

The first thing you see are the dunes.

So white in the February sun that they almost look like snow drifts except for the long slender green dune grass waving gently in the breeze.

Beyond the dunes the sunlit water shimmers clear out to the horizon.

It seems like it could go on forever.

In distance and in time.

And now that I thought of it, it most certainly would go on regardless of whether Eros struck or not.

With time the dust in the atmosphere would settle and the nuclear winter would abate.

Things would eventually go back to the way they'd been.

Only humans and a number of other large mammals wouldn't be there to see it.

The road to the beach ended in an asphalt parking lot covered with a fine layer of windblown sand.

I was surprised to find half a dozen vehicles parked in the spots closest to the dunes.

Most of them fairly decrepit.

The sort of cars surfers drive.

Cracked windshields.

Rusted-out mufflers wired to undercarriages.

Faded sun-bleached paint on roofs, hoods, and trunks.

Rear bumpers covered with a pox of stickers and decals advertising wet suits, boards, and surf wax.

Nestled among these rusted beasts was a familiar-looking motorcycle.

I brought my car to a stop.

The sun shone in through my shatterproof windshield.

The reflection glaring off the odd piece of uncorroded chrome made me squint.

Deep in the recesses of my consciousness, the question What am I doing here? began to beat repeatedly like a drum.

I had no answer.

I, Allegra Hanover, who knew precisely why I did everything.

Whose every waking moment was planned.

Whose every action made sense.

Was dangling without a net.

I felt like I was walking to the end of a plank.

Below me was the sea of uncertainty.

Would I jump?

I don't know how long I sat in my car.

Strange, unconnected thoughts flitted through my mind.

Years ago, during the Tickle Me Elmo doll craze, a woman in Springfield, Missouri, was standing in her kitchen when she heard the doorbell ring.

She went to answer it.

Outside stood a man.

In one hand he held an empty beer bottle by the neck.

In the other hand he held the woman's kitten by the neck.

The man said he wanted a Tickle Me Elmo doll.

The woman said she didn't have one.

The man turned and headed for his car, shouting over his shoulder that she wouldn't get her kitten back until she gave him Tickle Me Elmo.

As the horrified woman watched, the man got in his car and drove away.

She never saw the man or her kitten again.

Did that make sense?

Of course not.

So why did I keep insisting that everything had to make sense?

I got out of the car.

It was chillier at the beach, but, thankfully, there was barely any wind.

I opened the trunk and took out a jacket (I had been a good Brownie. I was always prepared).

But didn't move from behind the car.

I could feel The Need To Make Sense creeping up on me.

Paralyzing me.

But wait!

Did a man who abducted kittens and demanded Tickle Me Elmo dolls make sense?

Did a killer asteroid coming out of nowhere make sense?

How about thermonuclear war?

Or school dress codes?

Like a person learning to walk again after a serious injury, I took one tenuous step forward.

It didn't make sense.

But I did it.

Emboldened by my newfound ability to rise up against reason, I took another step.

And then another.

Until I reached the end of the parking lot.

And climbed up on the dune.

Where I stood among the softly swaying dune grass.

And beheld one of the strangest sights I had ever seen.

11

"I'LL NOT LISTEN TO REASON...REASON ALWAYS MEANS
WHAT SOMEONE ELSE HAS GOT TO SAY."
—*Elizabeth Clighorn Gaskell*

To recap: I was standing atop a dune. Part of a long line
of dunes that, except for a few public buildings and beach
houses, stretched to my right and left as far as I could see.

Spread out before me was the water.

Nestled like a soft white lining between the water and
the dunes was the thin strip of off-white sand we call
beach.

And it was there that I beheld the sight I found so
strange.

Dotting the beach like inexplicable artifacts left by
some ancient, long vanished civilization were surfboards
planted rear end first in the sand and standing upright
like totems to the surfing gods.

Huddled humbly beside the boards, either alone or in
groups of twos and threes, were surfers.

Each and every one of them staring, unmoving, out to sea.

I stood on the dune, slightly mesmerized by the sight.

Uncertain of what to do.

Nervous that, if I walked down to the beach, I would enter an alien land inhabited by a foreign culture.

It would be so easy to turn around, get back in my car, and leave.

Back to my safe, antiseptic, shatterproof world.

But did that make sense?

I studied the surfers more closely.

Directly in front of me was a group of three.

Twenty-five yards to their left were two more.

Squatting in the sand twenty-five yards to their left was a lone surfer.

With a bright yellow and green surfboard.

It was Andros.

I started toward him.

On the downward slope of the dune my shoes filled with sand.

I took them off.

On the surface the sand felt warm.

But when my bare feet sank into it, it felt surprisingly cold.

Like so many people I knew.

Warm on the surface, cold underneath.

And what about Andros?

I reached the bottom of the dunes and started to cross the beach.

At water's edge the little waves curled gently then lapped against the shore, making no more noise than the splash you'd hear while doing the dishes.

But there was a great deal of noise in my head.

Vast regions of my brain were sounding alarms, launching bright red flares, and blaring out warnings to cease and desist.

Stop and retreat!

Back off before it was too late!

Vamoose!

And yet I marched onward.

Andros sat on the sand, facing the water, unaware of me.

He was wearing a tattered grayish wet suit with seams coming undone in various places.

Over it he wore a baggy gray sweatshirt with a number of holes and rips.

He'd draped his leather motorcycle jacket over his shoulders.

He also wore a frayed baseball hat and sunglasses.

I stopped a few feet to his right.

He turned his head almost imperceptibly.

I couldn't see his eyes behind the sunglasses, but I knew he was studying me.

Then he turned and faced the sea once more.

I waited, my feet chilled by the cold sand, until it began to seem silly.

After all, hadn't Andros come to my car that morning to ask if I knew that the world was about to end?

Why could he talk then and not now?

"Uh, excuse me," I said.

"Shhh..." He brought his finger to his lips and shushed me.

"Why?" I whispered.

"I think I can hear it," he whispered back.

"Hear what?" I asked, still keeping my voice low.

"The asteroid."

"Uh...I don't think so."

"Why not?" he asked.

"Because it's in space," I explained. "And space is a vacuum. Sound waves can't travel in a vacuum."

Andros's broad high forehead wrinkled. "What about *Star Wars*?"

"Sound effects," I answered.

His head bobbed up and down. "Interesting."

"Not really," I said. "One is basic physics. The other, basic Hollywood."

"Not that," he said.

"Not what?"

"Not physics or Hollywood," he replied. "You."

"Me?"

"The way you think."

"Why, thank you." I took it as a compliment.

"Rigid channels," he said.

"Huh?"

"I can see the way you think," he explained. "The rigidity of your thought channels. Let me give you an example. How many ways are there to make a right turn?"

"What?"

"How many ways are there to make a right turn?" he repeated.

"There's only one," I answered. "You make a right turn by making a right turn."

"What about making three lefts?" he asked.

Three lefts?

He was correct, strictly speaking.

"But that's ridiculous!" I sputtered.

"Why?" he calmly asked.

"Because..."

"Because to you all square pegs have to go in square holes. Every question has one right answer. Everything is based on your one-dimensional interpretation of reality."

I had a feeling he was not being complimentary after all.

"How can you say that?" I asked. "You don't even know me."

"Hmmm..." He stared at the water.

"Okay, Mr. Multidimensional," I said. "I suppose you *can* hear the asteroid?"

"Maybe."

I waited for him to say something more, but it didn't come.

He seemed satisfied with "maybe."

And *maybe* I'd made a big mistake.

I was starting to have my doubts about Andros.

I was beginning to wonder if he'd ever spent any time in Springfield, Missouri, looking for a Tickle Me Elmo doll, or drilling holes in his skull.

I considered leaving.

Then remembered that I'd just performed a major friendectomy.

If I left, I'd really be lost.

And alone.

Now I saw what I'd foolishly done.

I'd burned my bridges.

I'd placed all my hopes in Andros.

No, not in Andros himself, but in the Andros I'd imagined him to be.

Not that I knew exactly what *that* Andros was either.

But he definitely wasn't *this* Andros.

The one I'd imagined was the blond, handsome, *silent* type.

Unimaginably wise and strong and solid.

Unimaginable, all right.

Small waves lapped at the sand.

Andros remained immobile.

So now what?

Did I get in the car and crawl back on my hands and knees begging forgiveness from Derman and Angie?

Forgiveness for *what?*

For not understanding how they could betray me?

Or did I stand there on the cold sand waiting for my toes to go numb while hoping that Andros would turn into the person I'd imagined he'd be?

"It's all a joke, you know," he said, still not taking his eyes off the horizon.

"What is?"

"This. That. Everything."

"The entire population of the earth perishing?" I asked.

He turned and looked up at me then, but all I saw was

the darkness of his sunglasses. "You think that's important?"

"As a matter of fact, yes, I do."

"It's not."

"How can you say that?" I asked. "You're talking about billions of lives."

"You know what Pascal said?" he asked.

"Who?"

"Blaise Pascal, seventeenth-century French philosopher and mathematician. Pascal's law is named after him. You know Pascal's law?"

I shook my head, but felt infinitely better.

We had found common ground.

Even if it was seventeenth-century French philosophy.

It was solid, scholarly.

Something you learned in school.

Something you could read in a book.

No more listening for silent killer asteroids.

Andros waved his hand toward the sea. "Pascal's law states that liquid in a vessel carries pressures equally in all directions. It's the basis for how a hydraulic jack works."

"Glad to hear it." I saw no reason to mention that I wouldn't know a hydraulic jack if it leaped out of the sand and smacked me on the head. "But what does that have to do with the billions of people who will die if this asteroid hits?"

"Later in life Pascal turned to religion," Andros explained. "Then he wrote: 'The natural misfortune of our mortal and feeble condition is so wretched that when we consider it closely, nothing can console us.'"

"Well, that was his opinion," I replied.

"Pascal also believed that faith is a sounder guide than reason," Andros went on. "He believed there were limitations to reason, but no limitation to faith."

"What does that have to do with humanity perishing?" I asked.

"It all has to do with what you believe in," Andros replied. "You believe it matters. I don't."

"How can you not think it matters?" I asked.

"Because it doesn't. Not when it was all an accident to begin with."

"What was?"

"Life," he said.

Less than two minutes into my first real conversation with Andros Bliss, and we were discussing the meaning of life.

It could have been worse.

I guess.

But I had other things in mind.

"I hate to bring this back to the mundane," I said, "but you haven't even asked me what I'm doing here."

"Doesn't matter."

"Oh, well, thanks for caring." I felt slighted.

Without looking at me, Andros said, "Why do you take everything personally?"

"You could be curious." I pouted.

"It doesn't matter."

"Please stop saying that," I said. "It really irks me. It may even be insulting, but I have to think about it."

"It wouldn't matter who was here," Andros said. "Not the president of the United States or the king of the world."

"Why not?"

"Because it wouldn't. It's all disharmonious conjunctions."

"You're really not curious about why I'm here?" I asked.

Andros didn't answer.

"Then why did you come over to my car this morning and tell me the world was ending?"

"I felt like it," Andros said.

"You felt like it," I repeated. "And you always do just what you feel like doing?"

"Pretty much."

I wasn't sure I believed him.

But it was interesting anyway.

Because I almost *never* did what I felt like doing.

"But why me?" I asked. "Why not someone else?"

I braced myself, expecting him to answer that there was no reason.

That it was purely arbitrary.

That he would have told a squirrel if he'd run into one.

Instead he said, "Because I wanted to be the one to tell you."

"Why?"

"Because I did."

"How did you know I didn't already know?"

"I saw you drive into the parking lot," he explained. "I saw the look on your face."

Hmmm...PERCEPTIVE! But still...

"You don't even know me," I said.

"I've seen you around."

Ah ha! Yahoo! Evidence of premeditation!

"Let me guess," I said. "You thought I was such a rigid person that you were just dying to see my reaction to something so totally out of my control?"

"No."

"Then why?"

"Because I felt like it."

I was starting to see a pattern. "Why do I have the feeling we're going around in circles?"

"Because you ask too many questions," he said. "You're trying to get answers when there aren't any. Why don't you just relax and let things happen?"

"But what's going to happen?" I asked.

Andros gave me a look.

"Oops." I caught myself. "I'm not supposed to ask."

"Especially the questions I can't answer." He winked. Cute.

"And there are absolutely no questions you feel like asking me," I said, trying not to make it sound like a question.

"There is one," Andros said. "What's your name?"

12

"THE HEART HAS ITS REASONS,
WHICH REASON KNOWS NOTHING OF."

—*Blaise Pascal*

Hello?

Did I hear him correctly?

Here I was standing on this chilly beach in the middle of February on what just might be the last day of the world with someone who didn't even know my name?

"How can you not know my name?" I asked.

"Easy," he answered, obviously enjoying my incredulity.

"I don't believe you," I said.

He was still smiling. "Can you spell egocentric?"

"Oh, really?" I shot back. "Can *you* spell dimwit?"

"Tsk, tsk." He shook his head. "Hostile."

"Would you mind wiping that smug smile off your face?" I asked.

"You can't stand it, can you?"

"No, I can't," I confirmed. "And truthfully, I don't believe it."

"Why not?"

"Because we go to school together."

"No, we don't," he said.

He had a point.

"Let me rephrase that," I said. "We go to school together when you choose to come to school."

"So?"

"So I know you know my name," I stated firmly.

Andros chuckled. "Okay, look, what's my name?"

"Andros Bliss."

He frowned and pointed at a group of surfers down the beach. "I'm not Andros. *He's* Andros."

What!? I stared down the beach.

Andros smiled again. "See?"

"See what?"

"For a second there you weren't sure," he said.

"This is ridiculous," I groused.

"Not really. You *think* I'm Andros, but you don't necessarily *believe* it. It goes back to what Pascal said. Reason will only get you so far. But belief will take you all the way."

What I wanted to do right then was get *all the way* out of there.

But I couldn't.

Something was making me stay.

Maybe it was that handsome, mocking smile.

Maybe it was that glimmering, teasing quality.

But mostly it was the lack of anyplace else to go.

"I still don't believe that you don't know my name," I said.

"Why not?" he asked.

"Because when you do choose to attend school, we go to the same school. We're in the same grade. We know people in common."

"Who?"

Hmmm...that was a tough one. Who *did* we know in common? I didn't know who his friends were. I didn't even know if he *had* friends. And he certainly didn't converse with my friends.

"Principal Dixon and Assistant Principal Rope," I said.

"That's like saying I should know your name because we both know who the president is," Andros said dismissively.

"Karl Luckowsky," I offered up next.

"Same difference."

I decided to trick him. "Allegra Hanover."

"Who?"

"Allegra Hanover. Class valedictorian. National Merit Scholarship finalist. President of the honor society. The first person in the history of Time Zone High to get eight hundreds on both SATs."

Andros shivered slightly. "She sounds scary."

I couldn't stand it any longer! "That's me, for God's sake!"

He studied me while I recovered from my little outburst. "Eight hundreds on *both* SATs?"

"Yes."

"That's an accomplishment."

"Thank you," I said. "And please don't tell me it's meaningless."

Andros shrugged. "You've done well in two of the seven kinds of intelligence. You said your name was Algra?"

"Allegra," I corrected him. "But everyone calls me Legs. And excuse me for saying this, but you're either intelligent or you're not."

"Okay."

We went silent again.

Andros seemed perfectly content to let the conversation die.

Meanwhile, dozens of questions poured through my mind.

I tried to resist them, but the onslaught was over-whelming.

Finally it became too much.

"Andros?"

"Hmmm?"

"Can I just ask one question?"

He grinned. "You just did."

"Okay," I sighed. "Can I ask one *more* question?"

"Sure."

"What are you doing here?"

He picked up some sand, then let it stream out of his fingers. "Just being."

"Right, I think I understand," I said. "But why are you just being here? Why not just be at the mall, or just be at a movie?"

"This is where I like to be," Andros replied.

It was puzzling.

On one level, I felt like we were just going around in circles.

But on another level, I felt like we'd actually made progress.

Toward what? I didn't know.

Then again, Andros would probably say we weren't *supposed* to know.

We weren't even supposed to wonder.

We were just supposed to be.

There on the cold sand at the beach.

I was trying to get comfortable with the concept of just being when Andros got up and walked down to the water's edge.

He stood there, just inches from the cold, clear winter sea, with his back to me.

Of course, I wondered why he'd done that.

Then I worked on not wondering why.

Then Andros shouted, *"Where is it?"*

I glanced at the other surfers up and down the beach.

Not one of them turned in our direction.

"Where is it?" Andros shouted again at the water.

The water didn't answer.

Then again, Andros didn't appear to expect an answer.

"Where is it?" he shouted yet again.

About a hundred yards down the beach, a surfer with a long brown ponytail stood up and sauntered to the water's edge.

"Where is it?" he shouted.

"Where is it?" yelled Andros.

They were soon joined by a few others.

It wasn't long before almost all the surfers were standing at the water's edge, bellowing at the sea like a pack of dogs howling at the moon.

A dozen voices up and down the beach.

All shouting *Where is it?* at the top of their lungs in no particular order or rhythm.

Normally, I would have concluded that they were all one taco short of a combination plate.

But I was trying, *really* trying, just to be.

"*Where is it?*"

"*Where*"

"*Is*"

"*It?*"

Andros turned away from the water's edge and came back up the beach toward me.

The other surfers continued to yell for a few moments more.

Then, one by one, they too turned away.

Until there was only one left at the water's edge.

Who shouted, "*Sorry doesn't walk the dog, honey!*"

And then returned to his board.

Andros sat down on the sand again and faced the water.

Acting as if nothing had happened.

It was driving me crazy.

"I'm sorry," I apologized. "I know I'm not supposed to ask, but I can't help it. It's my inquisitive nature."

"Just felt like it," Andros answered my question before I asked it.

"Of course," I said. "How dim of me not to think of that. But what I'm really dying to know is what *it* is. I mean, the *it* you've been referring to as in 'Where is *it*?' "

"The Big One," Andros answered.

13

"LIVE FAST, DIE YOUNG
AND HAVE A GOOD-LOOKING CORPSE."

—*John Derech*

The Big One...

"They say it could be six hundred feet high," Andros said.

"Come again?"

"The wave."

"Wave?"

"Caused by the asteroid. Six hundred feet is like a sixty-story building. It's like when you let go of a balloon and it's just a dot in the sky. It's the zenith, the ultimate surfing myth come true."

Speaking of waves, a ripple gastrointestinal discomfort washed through my lower regions. It was either fear or hunger. Possibly fear *of* hunger. But definitely not a hunger for fear. I had enough of that already.

"That's what you're all doing here?" I asked, trying to fend off the grumbling.

"Uh huh."

"Is it like the famous mountain climber who, when asked why he climbed the mountain, replied, 'Because it's there'?"

"You can't trivialize this," Andros replied solemnly.

"I'm just trying to understand," I said.

"Why do you have to understand?"

"Because I want to, I guess."

He leaned back and rested his elbows in the sand. "You can't. It's not about reason and understanding. It's about faith. You either have it or you don't."

The not-too-subtle implication being: I didn't.

"Is it possible?" I asked. "I mean, to actually surf this wave?"

"No one knows."

"What happens if you try and fail?"

"If there's a wave, it means the asteroid's hit," Andros replied.

"So it won't make a difference," I intuited.

"You got it."

"It's scary."

"Sure it is," Andros agreed.

"You're scared?" I asked.

"You'd have to be insane not to be."

"Then why?"

Andros stared at the ocean. "Gotta do it."

I tried to imagine the grandmother of all waves. As tall as a sixty-story building...

"In a weird way, it could be your salvation," I said.

Andros gave me a puzzled look.

"What I mean is, if you catch it, you could ride it all the way until it ended," I explained. "This thing of mass destruction could actually transport you to safety. It might just be an example of chaos theory."

Andros lowered his sunglasses and studied me with an inscrutable expression not unlike the one I'd seen on the face of the Reason Police officer who'd pulled me over for my illegal right turn on red.

He stood up and wiped off the sand. "Come on."

"Where are we going?" I asked.

"I heard your stomach rumble before," he said. "Hungry?"

It occurred to me that I was. "Is this an invitation?"

"Got any money?" he asked.

Some invitation.

"I'm paying for lunch?" I asked in my undying need for clarification. We were crossing the sandy parking lot. Andros was still wearing the wet suit under the ragged sweatshirt and leather jacket.

"If you want," he said.

"It's fine," I said. "I mean, I really don't care. I've got the money. And it wasn't like I was much of a saver even when the end of the world wasn't a possibility. But just out of curiosity, suppose I didn't have any money?"

"We wouldn't eat."

"It's that simple?"

Andros stopped and turned to me.

He was still wearing the sunglasses.

But I imagined his intense hazel green eyes, and felt an excited chill.

"It's only complicated if you make it complicated," he said. "Otherwise, it's simple."

"Right." I liked the force of his presence, but it made me nervous and uncertain. I tugged at the sleeve of his tattered sweatshirt and we started to walk again.

"Suppose I hadn't come along?" I asked.

"Not relevant."

"Of course." I was catching on more quickly now. "Because I *did* come along. And that's all that matters."

"Yup."

I hate to admit it, but the memory of the female angler fish darted through my mind.

True, the actual Andros, as opposed to my fantasy of him, was growing in stature and magnetism.

But I couldn't help wondering, was a male parasite attaching itself to me?

Oh, think, think, think, worry, worry, worry.

We were talking about lunch.

Not a lifetime together.

Could you imagine life with Andros?

"What are you doing today, Andros?"

"I don't know."

"You're just going to sit there?"

"I guess."

No, even if the silent maybe real killer asteroid Eros missed us, this afternoon did not portend a long-term relationship.

Andros stopped beside his motorcycle.

"So, er, I'll follow you," I said, glancing over at my car.

He scowled.

Oh, no! He didn't really think...

He *couldn't* actually believe...

That I'd go *on* that thing with him.

Andros just stood there studying me. Clearly he didn't understand that—provided we didn't all go *splat!* in a few hours—I had a future.

I had plans.

I'd worked incredibly hard in school.

In the fall I would be enrolled at one of our country's premiere learning institutions where I would have a dual major in Chinese and International Relations.

The great nation of China was going to unfold like a flower.

The opportunities...for cultural exchange...financial partnerships...joint research...were huge.

I wasn't about to give it all up for a brain hemorrhage.

As if he'd read my mind, Andros handed me his scratched red helmet.

My heart palpitated!

Such a touching gesture!

Just imagine. A little while ago he didn't even know my name, and yet now he was willing to sacrifice his own brain for mine.

I handed the helmet back.

Unless he could guarantee the safety of the *rest* of my body, I wasn't going to risk it.

"It's not far," he said, handing the helmet to me yet again.

"Most accidents happen within two miles of the home." I handed the helmet back one more time.

"We're nowhere near home." The helmet came back.

"I was extrapolating." The helmet *went* back.

Andros stared down at the helmet and pursed his lips in a tiny kiss of frustration.

"It's nothing personal," I said.

He slid the sunglasses up on his forehead and fixed me with his piercing hazel green eyes.

My heart reverberated. A wild herd of goose bumps stampeded down my arms.

"I know it's nothing personal," he agreed. "But you know what?"

"What?"

"I'd really like you to ride with me."

I'd never been on a motorcycle before.

The helmet was too large and slipped around on my head no matter how much I tightened the chin strap.

Seated behind Andros, I clung tightly to the leather jacket.

Can we talk about wind chill?

It was *freezing*!

Even with Andros blocking the bulk of the wind it was still ice cream headache cold.

Little rivulets of chilly air slipped up my sleeves, in and around under my jacket, and in through the side of the helmet.

The pitch of the engine grew higher as he twisted the hand grip back.

We were going much too fast.

I was frightened and mad.

Was Andros trying to scare me? Impress me?

If so, the only thing he was impressing me with was his stupidity.

Well, I wasn't about to stand for it. (Or, given the fact

that I was on the back of his motorcycle, *sit* for it).

If he wanted to show off and risk someone's life, let it be someone else's.

I stretched up, preparing to shout in his ear that he should either slow down or let me off.

That's when I noticed the speedometer needle hovering just below 25 mph...

That was odd.

I settled back down.

It *felt* like we were going *much* faster.

I would have guessed 65 or 70 mph at least.

And yet, looking off to the left and right, I perceived that we weren't passing things very fast at all.

I relaxed...just a little.

It still felt like a wild ride.

In more ways than one.

It wasn't long before Andros slowed down.

In what appeared to be the middle of nowhere.

On either side of the road were vast dull brown farm fields.

Broken rows of withered crops.

He turned the motorcycle down a pitted, bumpy dirt trail.

We proceeded slowly, bouncing through shallow pot-holes.

Winding around the deeper ones.

Stirring up a thin tail of dust.

Ahead I could see marshlands. The road was now lined with tall brown reeds and cattails. At the sound of the motorcycle, a red-winged blackbird took flight.

A weather-beaten gray shack appeared in the distance. It was built on stilts and seemed to be perched right on the edge of an inlet.

Without warning, a dented red pickup barreled past us, kicking up a cloud of dust. Through squinting eyes I saw a hand and a flapping green plaid shirt reach out of the window and wave.

Andros waved back.

In the back of the pickup, a large furry black dog with a patch of white and brown at its throat barked at us and wagged its tail.

The pickup was also headed for the shack on stilts.

There was no place else to go.

By the time we reached the dirt parking lot, the owner of the pickup, and his dog, had already gone up the weather-beaten stairs and inside. Andros held the motorcycle steady while I got off. I pulled off the helmet and shook out my hair.

The scent of frying food wafted out of a crooked metal pipe sticking out of the roof of the shack. But there was no sign indicating just what this establishment was.

Andros gestured for me to go up the wooden steps.

I went up and stopped at the weather-beaten gray door. On it were hand-painted words: No one under 21.

I glanced back quizzically at Andros, who reached past me to open the door.

"Past lives included," he said.

14

"WITHOUT ICE CREAM,
THERE IS CHAOS AND DARKNESS."

—*Don Kardong*

Inside the place was just as worn and weather-beaten as on the outside. I counted a dozen small tables covered with red and white checked plastic tablecloths, crowded with people of all ages. Along one wall was a bar, and along the other an open kitchen. The walls were covered with photographs of boats, little league teams, motorcycles, babies, and grinning men and women holding fish.

"This is stupid," a familiar voice said.

It was Dave Ignazzi. He and Chase Hammond were sitting at a table. Standing between them was Ray Neely. Piled on a plate in the middle of the table was a stack of cheeseburgers at least a foot and a half high.

The greasy buns and dripping yellow cheese leaned precariously, threatening to topple over at any moment.

"I've waited all my life to do this," Ray announced,

placing one last cheeseburger on the tilting pile. "Behold! The Leaning Tower of Cheeza!"

"Great," Dave muttered. "Can we go find some girls now?"

Andros and I moved through the room. A variety of people sat at the other tables. One or two wore jackets and ties, but most were in sweaters and shirts. To be honest, I had expected more of your basic laboring types. There were a few, but like the suits, they were in the minority.

A woman sitting alone at a table waved to Andros. I recognized the green plaid shirt. She was the driver of the pickup that had passed us. Sure enough, the large black dog lay on the floor beside her chair.

Andros started toward her and I followed.

She had an open, friendly face.

No makeup.

Her long straight brown hair was pulled back in a ponytail.

She was older than us. Not our parents' age, but somewhere in between.

"Hey, stranger," she said to Andros, pulling back a chair for him.

"Hi, Nat." Andros sat down and gestured for me to do the same.

Nat gave me a warm smile. "Hi."

"This is Allegra," Andros said.

"I like that name," the woman said. "My name's Natalie, but people call me Nat." She turned back to Andros. "Long time no see. Whatcha been doing?"

"The usual. Waiting for the world to end." Andros winked.

"What's the latest?" Nat asked.

"You got me," Andros replied. "I've been at the beach."

I looked around for a television set turned to the news, or at very least, a radio.

Nada. Here in this shack on stilts in the marshlands we were about as far from the information superhighway as you could get.

A waitress with a green pad and a pen sidled up to our table. She was dressed in black and had long curly black hair and a gold nose ring.

"Heard anything, Em?" Nat asked her.

"About the asteroid?" The waitress absently curled some hair around her finger. "Either happens or it doesn't. Whatcha having?"

How casual! You would have thought the possibility of the world ending was an everyday occurrence.

"What's the special?" asked Nat.

"Ice-cream sundae," replied Em, the waitress.

"For lunch?" I blurted.

"Could be the last day of your life, hon," the waitress replied. "You really worried about calories?"

She had a point. We decided on the sundaes. Andros and Nat went for the hot fudge, but I held out for butterscotch with sprinkles. A little while later I found myself staring down at one of the most delicious-looking lunches I'd ever seen.

I slid a spoonful of vanilla ice cream, butterscotch syrup, and sprinkles into my mouth and let it all melt on my tongue. Feeling emboldened by the absurdity of the circumstances, I took the most unusual step of revealing a little bit of my feelings.

"Am I the only one around here who seems to feel ever so slightly panicked by all this?" I asked.

"On the contrary," Nat replied. "I think you're part of the vast majority. Look around."

I saw what she meant. With the exception of the Leaning Tower of Cheeza table, almost everyone was eating an ice-cream sundae.

Three pretty girls came in.

All sounds emanating from the vicinity of Neely-Hammond-Ignazzi instantly ceased.

The girls took a table not far from them.

"Our prayers have been answered!" I heard Dave Ignazzi whisper. "This could be our big chance!"

The world might be ending, but some things would never change.

Andros and I made pleasant conversation with Nat about the weather, how tasty the sundaes were, the expanding nature of the universe, and the fact that in the Arctic the sun sometimes appears to be square.

Then Nat looked at her watch and said she had to go.

We told each other how nice it was to have met, and she gave Andros a kiss on the cheek.

She told Lucy, her furry black dog, that they were leaving.

Lucy got up and followed her out the door.

"Who is she?" I asked Andros when she was gone.

The fine lines in Andros's forehead furrowed. "She's Nat."

"Yes, but I mean, how do you know her? What does she do? Where does she come from?"

He gazed at the door, as if trying to picture her again. "I don't know. The only time I see her is here when I come for lunch. We just talk."

"And you don't know anything about her?" I asked.

"She's a nice person to have lunch with," Andros said.

Could life really be so simple?

15

"IF OLIVE OIL COMES FROM OLIVES,
AND PEANUT OIL COMES FROM PEANUTS,
WHERE DOES BABY OIL COME FROM?"

—*Ray Neely*

Lunch over, we went down the weather-beaten steps and out to the parking lot.

Andros held the scratched motorcycle helmet toward me.

I stared at it, then at him.

"Listen, Andros," I said. "I've been trying really hard just to be in the moment and not worry about anything, you know?"

"Okay."

"And I've worked really hard at not asking dumb questions," I added.

"Uh huh."

"I mean, I hope you can understand how unnatural it is for me to behave this way."

"Right."

"But before I put this helmet on and get back on your motorcycle, there's something I really need to know."

"Okay."

"Where are we going next?"

"The beach."

"For how long?"

"As long as it takes."

"Till the big one either comes or doesn't?"

Andros nodded.

"That's not supposed to happen until tomorrow morning just around dawn."

"Yeah."

"So you want to stay at the beach *all night?*"

"Sure."

I was beginning to understand what he meant by my having rigid channels of thought.

"You've done that before?" I asked. "Spent the night at the beach?"

"Plenty of times."

"In the middle of winter?"

Andros gazed off into the distance and then back at me. "We'll build a fire."

A fire?

I admit this cast a whole new light (ha!) on the somewhat frigid, sandy possibilities for the evening. My mind was flooded with cinematic images of couples nestled closely together around a fire on the sand.

Faces brightened by the dancing flames.

Listening to beach music.

Roasting hot dogs on sticks.

But there was one thing all those beach movies never

explained: Where did you go when you needed to use the bathroom?

"I can't," I said, at the very same moment hoping that Andros would mount a persuasive argument and convince me that I could.

But he only looked down at the loose rocks and dusty potholes in the parking lot—and said not a word.

"It's just not me," I tried to explain.

"After tomorrow morning it may not matter who you are."

"But right now it does," I said. "And I can only go by what I am now. Otherwise, I wouldn't know what to be."

Andros took a deep breath and let it out slowly, as if he'd inhaled expectation, and exhaled regret. "I'll take you back to your car."

I know of three sports that can be won by going backward.

Crew.

Backstroke.

Tug of war.

I also knew that I was going backward.

Back to the beach.

Back to my car.

Back to my safe, antiseptic, shatterproof life.

Backing away from excitement, emotion, and risk.

Backing away from Andros.

I felt a deep sense of regret and disappointment.

What can I say?

The philosophers tell us to be true to thine own self.

There were lots of ways I could picture thine own self spending the coming night, perhaps my last on the earth.

But being at the beach without a clean port-a-potty wasn't one of them.

We stopped next to my car in the parking lot. I got off the motorcycle and handed the helmet to Andros.

While I was disappointed that he didn't try to convince me to stay, I was impressed that he'd acted like such a gentleman.

"It's been really interesting," I said.

He gazed back silently, his eyes inscrutable.

The motorcycle engine idled softly.

I felt like my emotions were at idle too.

"I hope you're not mad." I spoke with sincerity. "If it's any consolation, I think you're really charming and charismatic in an offbeat sort of way...I mean, if things were different..."

My country for a clean port-a-potty!

Andros remained expressionless.

I knew I was blathering like an idiot.

Parting is such sweet sorrow.

This wasn't the way I wanted him to remember me as he surfed boldly away on that grandmother of all waves.

I stretched up on my toes and kissed him on his gristled cheek.

Then turned away.

Andros kicked the motorcycle into gear and rode across the parking lot to the edge of the dunes.

I sat in my car and watched him.

Was my regret intensifying like a tropical depression on its way to hurricane strength?

Yes.

Was my temptation to stay at the beach magnifying like the Hubble Space Telescope as it climbed into orbit?

Yes.

Then what was *really* stopping me from staying?

Just me, a reasonably attractive young woman, and a dozen scruffy male surfers thinking it might be their last night on earth?

I don't think so...

I put the key in the ignition and turned it.

Nothing happened.

16

"WHAT A FINE COMEDY THIS WORLD WOULD BE
IF ONE DID NOT PLAY A PART IN IT."

—*Diderot*

Now what?

What cosmic joke was this?

The windows of my trusty little car might not have worked, the radio might not have played, but it had always started.

Why wouldn't it start now?

I kept turning the key.

Nothing happened.

Not a click.

Not a whine.

Not a snap, crackle, or pop.

Life certainly knew how to catch you off guard.

Killer asteroids...

Guys you couldn't make sense of...

Cars that wouldn't start...

I got out and stood for a moment in the parking lot. The sun was beginning to tilt into the west, casting an unusually crisp yellowish light across the dunes. I was struck by the contrast of brightness and shadow. The contrast between what is known and what is unknown.

What did I know? Not much.

I knew how to write an essay, and how to find a cosine. I knew who'd signed the Declaration of Independence and what the nitrogen cycle was. I knew how to say hello in Chinese and what the Boxer Rebellion had been about.

Did I know if the killer asteroid named Eros was real? No.

Did I know if Andros was the right kind of guy for me? No.

Did I know how to fix a car that wouldn't start? No.

Thank God I knew how to ask for help.

Surfers struck me as resourceful types.

One would probably know how to start my car.

At the very worst I would ask Andros for a ride home.

I felt fairly confident that he'd do it.

After all, he'd still be able to get back to the beach in plenty of time to catch the wave to end all waves.

I walked across the parking lot and climbed up on the dune.

A new sight met my eyes.

The surfers were now gathered in a circle beside a black van someone had driven down to the water's edge.

I spotted Andros in the circle and started down the dune toward him.

As I crossed the beach heads began to turn.

Eyes became riveted on me.

A dozen grungy male surfers thinking it might be their last night on earth...

A nervousness began to pool up inside me, and I felt only a tiny mist of relief when Andros pushed himself up off the sand and met me halfway.

"My car won't start," I said.

Andros didn't answer. We started to walk back up the beach. I felt like an idiot. Surely one of the most awkward things in life is making a big deal about saying good-bye, only to discover some pressing need to talk to that person a moment later.

Again the nervous urge to blather percolated out of my gut and into my throat. "I really don't understand it. It always starts."

"It's okay," Andros said in a way that laid to rest any need for further explanation.

We arrived at my car and he got in.

I'd left the keys in it.

It wasn't like it could be stolen.

Andros turned the key once, then got out of the car.

Without a word, he opened the hood. "Battery's gone."

I looked in. To be honest, I couldn't tell that anything was missing until he pointed at two thick greasy cables ending in rounded pieces of metal.

"Your battery usually sits between those two cables," he said.

I stared into the greasy, sooty insides of my car.

My battery was gone.

Had it decided to leave on its own free will?

Having heard that the end of the world might be imminent, had it undone the cables that bound it and run off for a last ditch jolt?

What a shocking (ha!) thought!

"Someone took it?" I asked.

Andros looked back toward the dunes. "Come with me."

"I took it," a surfer named Tyler acknowledged without the slightest hint of remorse.

Tyler was tall and sinewy with long straight brown hair pulled loosely into a ponytail. Like the others, he was dressed in a frayed wet suit with various layers of tattered clothes over it. Numerous beads were woven into a hemp necklace around his neck. I'd never seen him before; he seemed older; beyond high school.

He was standing beside the black van, which, I gathered, he owned.

The rest of the surfers were still sitting in the circle, but they were listening.

"Why?" I asked.

The van was facing the water. Tyler opened the back doors. Inside was a mattress, several dingy, balled-up blankets, various raggy-looking towels, and five wired together rectangular black boxes about the size of toaster ovens.

They were, I gathered, car batteries.

Including mine.

"For light," Tyler explained, pointing to a rack of lights mounted on a bar above the roof of the van.

Meanwhile, Andros stood by silently.

"I don't understand," I said.

"For the Big One," Tyler said. "If it comes in the dark, we have to see it."

"But I need it," I said. "I can't get home without it."

"Sorry."

I turned to Andros and gave him a pleading look.

"It's the will of the majority," he informed me in a solemn tone.

Andros said he'd give me a ride home. A few moments later we were back in the parking lot, getting on the motorcycle.

I was starting to feel like an old hand at this.

But I gazed longingly at my car and its shatterproof windows.

Although it was only symbolic, I felt like I was leaving my last bit of protection behind.

Without it I was vulnerable. Still in control (I hoped!) but not protected.

Anything could happen now.

17

"WHAT DOES IT MEAN WHEN WE PARK IN
DRIVEWAYS AND DRIVE ON PARKWAYS?"

—*Dave Ignazzi*

Derman was sitting at the foot of my driveway when
Andros and I rode up.

"Think I could go inside and use the facilities?" Andros
asked as we got off the motorcycle.

"Of course." I turned to Derman. "Be right back."

I let Andros in the house, then went back outside.

Derman was still sitting at the curb.

I sat down beside him.

"I knew it," he said.

"Knew what?" I asked.

"That if I waited here sooner or later you'd show up,
with him."

"Is it another one of the things you visualized?" I
asked.

Derman nodded. "You love him, don't you?"

"It's not what you think."

Derman rolled his eyes in disbelief.

"Wait a minute," I said. "You have a lot of nerve. Who are you to pass judgment when you profess undying love to me and then snake my best friend behind my back?"

"*That's* not what *you* think," Derman countered.

"Oh, please," I groaned dismissively. "Angie's been all over cyberspace trying to find out if she's still a virgin."

Derman shrugged. "So what's with Mr. Motorcycle?"

I explained that he'd just dropped me off and would be heading back to the beach shortly.

"Heard anything new?" I asked.

"Not really," Derman replied. "The government keeps insisting it's not happening. All kinds of people on the Internet keep insisting it *is* happening. The media keeps reporting both sides. The Christian fundamentalists say it's a warning to the liberals from God. The environmentalists say it's nature's revenge for all the damage we've done. The Muslims say it's the wrath of Allah. The UFO people say it's an alien sneak attack. And there's a guy in Fargo, North Dakota, who insists it's all because McDonald's raised the price of the Egg McMuffin."

The front door opened and Andros came out, a grim expression on his finely chiseled, stubbly face.

Derman stood up and extended his hand. "Hi, I'm Derman Bloom. I've seen you at school."

Andros shook his hand.

"I'm deeply in love with Legs," Derman said. "But it's been clear to me for some time that the feeling wasn't mutual."

"I hear you," replied Andros.

"I just want you to know that, given the current circumstances, I have no hard feelings," Derman said.

"I appreciate that," replied Andros.

"Hello!" I waved. "Do I have anything to say about this?"

Andros and Derman both gave me blank looks.

Then Angie drove up.

"What's this all about?" She got out of her car.

"Showdown at the End of the World Corral," Derman answered with a smirk.

"Funny you should say that," Angie replied. "I just heard that Jason Rooney is having an End of the World party tonight. Everyone's invited."

"I'll pass," Derman said.

Angie gave Andros another look.

"Angie Sunberg, this is Andros Bliss," I said. "He just gave me a ride home from the beach."

"The beach?" Angie raised her eyebrows.

"They're waiting for the Big One," I explained.

"The Big One," Angie repeated, aiming a quizzical glance at Derman, as if implying that I was losing my screws.

Derman yawned.

Angie also yawned.

"I wish you two would stop doing that," I said.

My two former closest friends shared a guilty look.

No one said anything.

There in my driveway were the major players in my life.

Andros. Derman. Angie.

"Maybe we should have a party of our own," I suggested.

That brought Angie back into focus.

"I've decided it didn't happen," she announced.

"What?" Derman responded quickly.

"Third law of virginity," Angie stated like a lawyer referring to precedent.

"What?" Derman again said.

"Everyone deserves a second chance." This came, most unexpectedly, from Andros.

The rest of us stared at him in amazed disbelief.

"How do you know about *that?*" I asked.

Andros screwed up his face as if trying to remember. "Heard it somewhere."

"Do *you* believe it?" Angie asked him hopefully.

He nodded. "It's a disharmonious conjunction of an endotruth and an unrule."

"What?" Derman seemed to be stuck on that word.

"An endotruth is what's known inside, but not outside a culture," Andros explained. "And exotruth is just the opposite. It's what the people outside the culture think is happening inside."

"You mean, like body piercing?" I asked. "Inside the culture people know it's just a form of identification for individuals with similar outlooks. But outside the culture people think it means you're some kind of deviant."

"You got it," Andros said.

"So you're saying that what may appear to be a loss of virginity to those on the outside, isn't necessarily a loss of virginity to those on the inside?" Angie asked.

"Right."

"But who's on the inside and who's on the outside?" Derman asked.

"Whoever chooses to be," Andros answered.

"No." Derman shook his head. "I'm sorry, but that doesn't cut it. Remember Heaven's Gate? That group of crazies who committed suicide because they thought an alien spaceship hiding behind the Comet Hale-Bop was coming to take their souls away?"

"So?" Andros said.

"The endotruth within the group was that the spaceship was really there," Derman argued. "But the exotruth...that is, what all the *rest* of us knew to be true, was that there was no spaceship and that the Heaven's Gate people were just a bunch of grape-nut flakes."

"How do you know?" Andros asked.

Derman's jaw dropped. "You're not serious."

"Hey, Mr. Smart Guy," I said. "People used to believe that politicians worked for the good of the masses."

"And that Rock Hudson was straight," added Angie.

"And that the potato chips at the top of the bag tasted better than the ones on the bottom," I said.

"They do," said Angie.

"All exotruths," Andros said.

Derman raised his hand as if we were in school, and in a voice seething with mocking insolence said, "I disagree, Mr. Motorcycle Man."

"You're just not in the culture," Angie accused him.

"No, it's not that," Derman said. "It's just that the world may end in less than twenty-four hours and we're standing around arguing about stupid concepts."

"Not stupid to me," Angie insisted.

"What if we're all dead?" Derman asked.

"What if we're not?" she shot back.

"You know, in one way, Derman is right," I said. "You both still betrayed me."

"That's where *you're* wrong," Derman replied. "That's the example of the exotruth. Meanwhile, the endotruth is something entirely different."

I gave Angie a probing look.

She diverted her eyes.

I turned back to Derman. "Well, *something* happened, and whatever it was, it directly contradicts your assertion that you are 'deeply and madly' in love with me."

"No," Derman insisted.

"Yes," I said.

"Excuse me," said Andros.

"What?" I turned to him.

He took me in his arms and kissed me.

"THE OCEAN IS A PLACE OF PARADOXES."

—*Rachel Carson*

I was rather proud of myself.

Transitions have never been easy for me.

Especially unexpected transitions.

I like to have time to prepare.

But in this case I suddenly and quite unexpectedly found myself in Andros's arms, his lips pressed against mine, our bodies clinging to each other, our eyes closed (at least, mine were).

He smelled leathery.

My heart was beating very fast and I felt like I'd suddenly developed a fever.

An extremely pleasant fever.

I found myself thinking that I was glad he wasn't shorter than me.

I've always imagined that it would be awkward to kiss someone shorter.

I sincerely believe that when kissing in a standing position, women are made to kiss UP and men are made to kiss DOWN.

I could only guess that it might be different in other positions.

I didn't know, actually.

It wasn't something I'd ever experienced.

The only kissing I'd ever done had been standing up.

Sort of kindergarten, kissing-wise.

I guess you could say that as far as my education at kissing school was concerned, I'd been left back.

Potty training for life...

I can't say that I'd been consciously concerned about catching up.

But I did like kissing Andros.

A lot.

Several years ago in Warsaw, Poland, three armed burglars broke into the apartment of a pregnant woman. While one of them held a gun on the woman, the other two burgled the place.

In the middle of this, the woman informed the men that she was going into labor.

The three robbers interrupted their robbery, drove the woman to a hospital so she could have her baby, then returned to the apartment and finished robbing it.

It's chaos theory again.

There can be beauty in the midst of tragedy, poignancy

in the midst of fear, warmth in the midst of devastation.

I can't tell you how long Andros and I kissed, but it went on for quite a while. There was something extremely nice about being connected to him in that particular manner.

I just wanted it to last.

If the world was about to end, this was definitely the way I wanted to go.

"Ahem!" The sound of a clearing throat interrupted us.

Still clinging to each other, Andros and I turned to find Derman and Angie with their arms crossed.

"Sorry to interrupt the PDA." Derman sounded irritated. "It's just that I need a little closure here before I go off and wait for the world to end."

To my surprise and consternation, Andros backed away from me. "I understand."

Derman turned to me. "I just want you to know that no matter what happened with Angie last night, I love you. I've loved you for a long time."

I turned and looked at Angie for her reaction.

She sort of shrugged, as if she were basically indifferent to his statement.

Next I looked at Andros.

He fixed me with those intense hazel green eyes and said, "I'd really like you to come back to the beach with me."

Once again images of snuggling beside a warm fire danced in my head.

I was too busy dreaming of more kisses to worry about the availability of port-a-potties.

I turned yet again to Derman and Angie.

Despite their betrayal.

Despite Angie's decision to deny the consummation of their betrayal, which in a way only proved that there'd been a betrayal in the first place.

Despite all of that...I still harbored great affection for them both.

"What are you two going to do?" I asked.

"The way you ask it implies that you think Derman and I are going to do something together," Angie replied with some acidity.

"Not necessarily," I said.

"Although, if Legs does go to the beach, it sort of leads us back to where we were last night," Derman said, sort of suggestively.

"Not a chance, buster," Angie snarled with chilling finality.

"Why don't you come to the beach?" Andros asked.

If I reacted too quickly, seemed slightly too aghast, can you blame me?

I had started to picture the perfect night to end all nights.

Andros and I snuggling together, alone, sharing our own little endotruths.

The last thing I wanted was Derman and Angie staring across the fire at us!

But Andros, who seemed to be growing progressively wiser, appeared to read my thoughts.

"If this is the end," he said, "you three can share the comfort of familiarity."

✻　★　✻

The phrase "strange bedfellows" came to mind.

That is, without any of the implications inherent in "bed."

Which left it just plain strange.

Imagine spending what might be the final hours of your life with:

1. Your former best friend, who has recently betrayed you with
2. your former boyfriend, who couldn't be happy about losing you to your
3. brand-new boyfriend, who may not actually be your boyfriend anyway.

After all, what *was* my relationship with Andros?

Yes, he'd kissed me.

Passionately, by my standards.

But I knew what he'd say if I asked.

It was just a kiss.

But why, Andros, why?

Because I felt like it.

But what does it mean, Andros?

Why does everything have to have a meaning?

Because it does.

To me, Allegra Hanover, *everything* had to have a meaning!

Things had to make sense!

Chaos theory was fine when we were talking about rats in a cage or the path a leaf takes when falling from a tree. Or even the course of a wayward asteroid wobbling through space.

But when it came to my fragile emotions, chaos theory could get stuffed!

This wasn't some cerebral "let's-impress-everyone-with-how-smart-we-are" classroom debate.

This was about feelings.

My feelings!

This was about emotions!

This was about...What if it didn't work out?

What if it was a huge cyberhoax like my mother contended? What if the world didn't end and there was a tomorrow and a day after that?

Then this was about...maybe getting hurt.

Being vulnerable and unprotected...

No shatterproof windows to hide behind...

Pain travels 350 feet per second.

I didn't want to get hurt.

But I did want Andros Bliss.

"Why not?" Derman asked.

"Why not what?" I'd lost track of what the question was.

"Why not go to the beach?" Derman said.

"Uh, it'll be cold," I stammered. "And you don't have any way of getting there."

Derman saw right through me. "You don't want us to go." He turned to Andros. "Excuse me for saying this, but she wants to be alone with you. She doesn't want us there interfering."

"It's a big beach," Andros said.

Angie grinned and winked. "Ooh-la-la!"

"That's not what he meant," I cried, then turned to Andros. "Is it?"

"I meant you don't have to be right on top of each other," Andros said.

"Why not?" Derman quipped suggestively.

"Don't be crass, Derman," I warned him.

"I'll be whatever I want," Derman shot back. "And I'll go whenever I want. Stop telling me what to do, Legs. We may have only a few hours to live. The regular rules don't apply anymore."

I turned to Angie. "You agree?"

She made a disagreeable face. "Isn't it cold at the beach?"

"We'll dress warm," Derman said. "We'll have a fire. Welcome to the End of the World clambake." He turned to me. "You and he can take a blanket and go off in the dark. You have my word that we won't sneak up with flashlights."

I felt my face turn hot and red. "Shut up, Derman."

At the same time I quickly glanced out of the corner of my eye to see how Andros took to the idea.

His face was impassive.

I got the feeling his thoughts were elsewhere.

Derman turned to Angie. "I'm going to the beach. I like the symbolism of it. A hundred million years ago life dragged itself out of the ocean and onto the shore. If this asteroid hits, it'll probably knock life back a hundred million years. Right back into the ocean."

"How do you know it won't kill everything in the ocean too?" Angie asked.

I raised my hand. "I can answer that. Theoretically, a prolonged nuclear winter would destroy all life on the earth's surface, since all life is either directly or indirectly dependent on the sun's energy. There are two exceptions. The first are certain viruses that have the ability to remain dormant and nearly indestructible for an extraordinarily long time until conditions change and become favorable, which would happen as the dust settled and the earth became warm again.

"The second exception is the recent discovery of a whole new ecosystem at the bottom of the ocean, which derives its energy from heat released from deep inside the earth."

"You mean, like tube worms and stuff?" Derman asked.

"Yes," I replied. "There's a whole food chain down there in the dark that mimics the one we know up here. At the bottom of our food chain are plankton, which live in the oceans and get energy from the sun. But at the bottom of the other food chain are chemosynthetic microbes that live off heat and hydrogen sulfides released from inside the earth."

"That don't need sunlight to live?" Angie asked.

"Yeah, I've read about that," Derman said. "It's extremely cool because it opens whole new possibilities for life on other planets. See, if life can exist at the bottom of the ocean, in total darkness and in extremely high heat, and survive on sulfur compounds that are otherwise totally poisonous to every creature living on earth's surface, it means life could exist on a lot of planets that we previously thought were totally inhospitable. In fact, just about anywhere there's water, there can be life."

"Didn't I just read something about comets being made of ice?" Angie asked.

"Exactly," Derman said. "All over the universe comets smash into planets and leave water there. That's why we think there could be life on Mars and even on the moons of Jupiter."

We were interrupted by the low, throaty rumble of a motorcycle engine.

Without any of us noticing it, Andros had gotten on his motorcycle.

He was looking at me and waiting.

I looked back at Derman and Angie. "Sorry, guys. Interesting conversation, but I think it's time to go."

19

"POETRY HAS AS ITS SUBJECT THE HUMAN HEART.
WHEN ONE KNOWS POETRY WELL,
ONE UNDERSTANDS...THE REASONS GOVERNING ORDER
AND DISORDER IN THE WORLD."

—*Kamo Mabuchi*

By the time we got back to the beach, the sun had started to set. It still felt early in the day, but then, it was February.

As I got off Andros's motorcycle, I glanced over at my own batteryless car with its shatterproof windows and felt a vague yearning to be back inside its protective confines.

But what did it protect me from?

Had I deluded myself in thinking that my car offered any real shelter at all?

Was it some last vestige of magic childhood "let's pretend"?

I turned back and found Andros watching me.

Our eyes locked.

A shiver of fear and need, like nothing I had ever experienced, rippled through my entire being.

Whatever sense of yearning I felt was now aimed squarely at him.

He must have seen it in my eyes.

He stepped toward me.

And I toward him.

I can't begin to explain what drove me.

It was magnetic.

Biological.

Electric.

Genetic.

Instinctual.

I didn't stop to think about it.

I *couldn't* stop to think about it.

Andros came closer. Grizzled, lanky, an aura of nonchalant testosterone faintly glowing around him, as if he were some fabulous celluloid movie-star being.

He was just about to take me in his arms when...we heard the sound of sand crushing under car tires.

Dave Ignazzi's car rolled to a stop a few feet away.

Dave hopped out. "Where's the party?"

Chase Hammond got out of the passenger side and Ray Neely slowly emerged from the back.

"What party?" I replied.

Dave's forehead bunched up. "Here at the beach. There's supposed to be a party. These girls said they'd meet us."

"The girls from Arizona?" I arched an amused eyebrow.

"Nah, not them, the ones from the restaurant." Dave looked around, then back at me. "You're joking, right? They're here." He pointed at the cars parked over by the dunes.

"Not to my knowledge," I replied.

Dave's mouth fell open, a truly astonished look on his face.

"Not again," Ray groaned.

Dave turned back to his buddies, his palms facing upward in a helpless gesture. "I don't believe it!"

Chase Hammond shook his head wearily. "I believe it. The only thing I *don't* believe is that after all this time, I still listen to you."

"Way to go, Dave," Ray added caustically.

Dave dashed across the parking lot, climbed the dunes, and scanned the beach.

"The guy never gives up," Chase smirked.

"The idea of having a beach party in February didn't strike you as a bit unlikely?" I asked.

"Sure it did," Chase replied.

"But so does the idea of getting smooshed by a giant asteroid," added Ray.

"I kind of wanted to come to the beach anyway," Chase said, then recited:

> The sea is calm tonight.
> The tide is full, the moon lies fair
> Upon the straits; on the French coast, the light
> Gleams, and is gone; the cliffs of England stand,
> Glimmering and vast, out in the tranquil bay....
> Listen! you hear the grating roar
> Of pebbles which the waves draw back, and fling,
> At their return, up the high strand,
> Begin, and cease, and then again begin,
> With tremulous cadence slow, and bring
> The eternal note of sadness in.

"Nice," Andros said with an approving bob of his head. "You write it?"

"Nah, some poet named Matthew Arnold," Chase answered.

Dave came back down the dune, shoulders slumped, head bowed. "Less than a day left to live and they're still scamming guys." He sounded disgusted. "Can't they think of anything better to do?"

"Can't we?" Ray asked.

"What are those surfers doing?" Dave asked Andros.

"Waiting for the Big One," Andros replied, then patiently explained about the grandmother of all waves.

"Whoa, sounds awesome!" Ray grinned maniacally.

"Too bad you don't surf, dimwit," Dave snarled with pent-up futility.

"Maybe not, but I skim." Ray went back to Dave's car and pulled a flat wooden skimboard out of the trunk. He carried it back to us.

"Okay if I hang with you guys?" he asked Andros.

"The beach is free," Andros replied.

"Cool." With skimboard in hand, Ray started across the parking lot.

"I think I'll hang here too," Chase said, and followed him.

Dave watched his friends start over the dunes. "I don't believe this," he muttered.

"What's not to believe?" I asked.

Dave narrowed his eyes and gave me a positively lethal look, then started to follow his friends.

✹ ★ ✸

During our absence, the surfers had collected driftwood to burn through the night. The dull, sun-bleached wood reminded me of bones.

Now in the grayness of dusk, they built a fire. The flames leaped up like a funeral pyre. A funeral for all the futures we might never have?

We sat in a circle around the orange, crackling glow.

I sat close to Andros, sharing the warmth.

Not far from us sat Chase, Dave, and Ray, who was busy waxing his skimboard.

Andros turned to me, the reflection of the flames dancing on his face. "What are you thinking?"

"Ninety-five percent of all the life-forms that ever existed on this planet are now extinct," I answered.

"Kind of puts things in perspective," said the pony-tailed surfer/battery thief named Tyler.

"Know what's really ironic?" Chase asked. "They say that the last time an asteroid hit, it wiped out the dinosaurs. And that's what allowed us to evolve from lesser mammals. Some scientists even think we might never have evolved into the dominant creatures on earth if the dinosaurs didn't kick off."

"Does that mean the dinosaurs just would have become smart?" Ray asked.

"I don't know how it works," Chase said. "Maybe the dinosaurs had no *reason* to become smart. They were already on top of the heap. Kind of like the alligator. Basically the same dumb beast for the last three hundred million years."

"If we become extinct because of this impact, what comes next?" Dave asked.

"I guess it depends on what can survive," Chase said.

"Cool," said Ray. "Like what do we think will survive? What'll be the next dominant life-form on earth?"

"Fish?" Dave guessed.

"Doubtful," I said. "The ocean food chains all come down to plankton and algae, both of which depend on sunlight."

"Then insects!" cried Ray. "Can't you just see it? Ten million years from now, big gnarly bugs with brains."

"Wonder what they'll look like," Chase mused.

Dave pointed through the dark. "Like that."

Wobbling toward us over the sand, in a somewhat off-balance manner, was a hulking shadowy creature resembling a huge *Far Side* beetle with a thick shell on its back.

In this case, a two-legged beetle.

A moment later Derman sank to his knees before the fire.

The huge shell was his backpack.

Angie came out of the shadows behind him.

"Planning to scale Everest?" I teased.

"Forget it!" Angie laughed ruefully. "You should have heard him moaning and groaning just climbing over a sand dune."

"It's heavy," Derman complained.

"He's got a pair of snowshoes in there," Angie said.

"It's stupid not to be prepared." Panting for breath, Derman defended himself. "I mean, nuclear winter's no picnic."

Ray got up and stopped behind the backpack. He lifted something off it. "Hip waders, man?"

"For the tidal wave," Derman replied.

"I don't think so," said Tyler.

Ray went skimboarding. Chase went back to Dave's car and got a glow-in-the-dark Frisbee. Then he, Dave, and a few surfers started to throw it around.

Those of us who remained by the fire—Andros, Derman, Angie, and me—watched the dull greenish disk sail through the night air, sometimes hovering and slowly dropping through the dark like a UFO.

"Here's something I bet you didn't know," I said. "The whole notion of UFOs didn't exist until 1947 when a man flying an airplane over the Cascade Mountains thought he saw a bunch of circular objects flying together in the sky."

"That's ridiculous," Derman argued. "The idea of alien visitors goes back centuries. Even the Aztecs had drawings of them. And in the 1930s, Orson Wells did that famous radio show about an alien attack that people thought was real."

"You didn't hear me correctly," I said. "I didn't say aliens, I said UFOs. Unidentified Flying Objects. Before 1947, when people talked about aliens from outer space, they were always identified as such. They were Martians or Venusians or whatever. But it never occurred to anyone to look up in the sky and see some flying object that wasn't from earth."

"Are you serious?" Angie asked.

"Yes. One person reported seeing a UFO and the idea got into people's heads, then you had millions of— Mmmmfff!"

Before I could say "sightings," Andros took my face in his rough hands and kissed me on the lips.

I kissed him back, of course, and felt the rough bristle of his jaw, and his fingers caressing my hair. His lips left mine and drifted slowly across my ear and down the side of my neck.

It was electric.

Passionate.

Blissful.

Somewhere in the distance I thought I heard Angie grumble, "I think I'm beginning to see a pattern here."

"Maybe intellectual conversation turns him on," Derman observed.

"Either that or it turns him off," replied Angie.

"I prefer on," Derman answered. "So what do you say?"

"I thought I heard you profess your undying love to Legs a few hours ago," Angie said.

"So?" Derman said. "Look what *that* got me."

I imagined him gesturing at Andros and me in our passionate embrace.

"Win some, lose some" was Angie's response.

"Or if you can't be with the one you love, why not love the one you're with?" Derman asked suggestively.

After which I most definitely heard the sound of a slap.

"Ow!" Derman yelped. "I was only kidding."

Andros and I continued to kiss.

I tried not to think.

Who wants to think when they're kissing by a fire on the beach on what just might be the final night of their lives?

But I couldn't help wondering why Andros chose these odd moments for romance.

Was Angie right?

Was there a direct relationship between my wandering off on some intellectual tangent and Andros's sudden bursts of amour?

Did it matter?

I must admit this was something I was starting to really enjoy.

The kissing, that is.

Each time we started, I wanted more.

It was like a stalking hunger that crept up unannounced.

Andros's lips were like some indescribably delicious junk food—chocolate, jelly beans, ice cream, and candy bars all rolled into one.

And the sensations it caused inside me were a fabulous sundae of warm mushiness melting atop glowing desire.

Still kissing, we started to sink down on the cool winter sand.

We might have been sinking down, but in the school of love I was rapidly moving up, out of kindergarten and into first, second, third grade.

"I'm not going to sit here and watch this." Derman's voice filtered through a thick haze of passion. "Let's go."

"Okay, but no tricks," Angie warned him.

"No tricks," Derman repeated in a defeated tone.

20

"WHEN HE SHALL DIE,
TAKE HIM AND CUT HIM OUT IN LITTLE STARS,
AND HE WILL MAKE THE FACE OF HEAVEN SO FINE
THAT ALL THE WORLD WILL BE IN LOVE WITH NIGHT."
—*William Shakespeare*

I lay nestled in the crook of Andros's arm.

He was lying on his back, staring up at the starry night sky.

A breeze had come up, fanning the driftwood fire and sending hot glowing sparks up the beach.

The surf was up.

Down at the water's edge the waves slapped and growled at the sand like angry animals unable to reach us.

"I think I disagree with Pascal," I said, mid-snuggle. "Our mortal and feeble condition may be wretched, but I find being with you very consoling."

"Yeah." Andros squeezed me.

Feeling an urge, but none of the reserve and caution that normally governed my every action, I stretched up and kissed him on his bristly cheek. "Do you mind talking?"

"No."

"Good. So...why me?"

He didn't hesitate. "Because you're smart and beautiful and I always sensed vast reserves of pent-up emotion inside you."

"Even though you didn't know my name?"

"What's a name? A label. A name isn't who we are."

"Who are we?" I asked.

"I already told you."

"Sorry, I forgot."

"Okay, but this is just what I think," he cautioned. "Just one person's opinion."

"The one person I'd most like to hear from," I said.

"Well..." Andros took a deep breath. "I think we're just an accident. A cosmic joke."

"What's so funny?" I asked.

"That we take ourselves so seriously. That we think life is so important. I mean, it is to each of us, but overall, in terms of time and space, in terms of the age and size of the universe, nothing we do or say, nothing that happens to us means anything."

"Back to Pascal?" I asked.

"Right."

"Then why bother?"

"There's only one reason I can think of." He propped himself up on his elbow and smiled down at me.

I reached up and pulled him down toward me.

One very worthwhile reason...

✦ ✦ ✦

Which made me wonder.

Had it all been a waste?

The hours, days...who are we kidding?...The *years* I'd spent in self-imposed emotional exile studying, learning, absorbing the useless bits and bytes of information that filled my brain.

And all the while my heart remained an empty vessel.

Or did the long wait only make this moment sweeter?

Was this the reward?

"I don't want to die," I whispered.

Clinging to Andros.

Mixing warm breaths.

Feeling more alive than I'd ever felt.

The irony of it.

To finally feel so alive, at what just might be the end of life.

"I'm scared," I whispered, knowing I'd never admitted such a thing to anyone before.

"Let's walk." Andros pushed himself up off the sand, then pulled me to my feet.

The fire still burned, but no one sat around it now.

Beyond the small circle of light it cast over the pitted, foot-scarred sand, we could see nothing but darkness and the outline of the van that contained my battery.

We started down the beach, hand in hand.

Walking along the waterline.

As we got away from the fire and our eyes adjusted, we could see the waves crashing in the moonlight, the white foam washing up the beach, and the dark wet wave prints left behind.

Way down the beach I saw a faint red glow brighten momentarily and then fade back to darkness. Someone was smoking.

Closer to us, three figures stood facing the waves. Chase Hammond had rolled up his pants and was standing ankle deep in the wash. Ray Neely stood behind him, wrapped in a blanket, his hair plastered down with seawater.

Dave Ignazzi stood farther back where it was dry.

We stopped beside him.

Rippling moonlight cut a wide swath out into the sea. Chase recited:

> *Ah, love, let us be true*
> *To one another! for the world, which seems*
> *To lie before us like a land of dreams,*
> *So various, so beautiful, so new,*
> *Hath really neither joy, nor love, nor light,*
> *Nor certitude, nor peace, nor help for pain;*
> *And we are here as on a darkling plain*
> *Swept with confused alarms of struggle and flight,*
> *Where ignorant armies clash by night.*

"More Matthew Arnold?" I asked.

"It's the only poem he knows," Dave answered. "He had to learn it for English."

"He's putting it to good use," observed Andros.

"Frankly, I could go for some Hendrix right about now," said Dave. "All Along the Watchtower."

"Definitely." Andros held out his hand and they slapped palms. Not the high five of athletic exuberance, but the low five of shared understanding.

Meanwhile, a dozen feet away, another wave washed over the bare ankles of Ray and Chase.

"Brrr, why are we doing this?" Ray asked through chattering teeth.

"Makes you feel alive," Chase replied.

"Make me feel *cold*," Ray said.

"You've got a point," admitted Chase.

They came back toward us.

"How much time left?" Chase asked.

Dave pressed a button on his watch and it glowed pale green. "Maybe six, seven hours."

"I want to go warm up." Ray was shivering.

"Yeah, and I'm hungry," said Dave.

The boys started back toward the fire.

Andros and I continued down the beach. The smell of salt water in the air. Our arms around each other. A small planet of two in its own orbit.

We didn't speak.

I'd lost the need.

Feeling oddly at peace.

As if I'd finally found what I was looking for.

There is a company in St. Louis, Missouri, that makes artificial dead-body scents.

But tell me, Matthew Arnold, is this the scent of love?

(Actually, the scientific explanation for scent of love is pheromones. A level of bio/chemical intra-human communication of which we are only vaguely aware.

So let's leave it that way.)

21

"HENCE IN A SEASON OF CALM WEATHER
THOUGH INLAND FAR WE BE,
OUR SOULS HAVE SIGHT OF THAT IMMORTAL SEA
WHICH BROUGHT US HITHER,
CAN IN A MOMENT TRAVEL THITHER,
AND SEE THE CHILDREN SPORT UPON THE SHORE.
AND HEAR THE MIGHTY WATERS ROLLING EVERMORE."

—*William Wordsworth*

The wind picked up even more.

In the moonlight the waves grew bigger and crashed with a roar. They were topped with white foam, and the air was filled with sea spray.

By the time Andros and I got back to the fire, the lights on the van's roof were ablaze, sending bright beams through the haze and spray and out to sea.

We could see the dark silhouettes of surfers bobbing in the swells. We watched as one of them kneeled on a board and began to scoop frantically ahead of a large cresting curl.

The wave caught him and he let out an exhilarated *Whoop!*

I waited for him to stand up and do whatever it was surfers were supposed to do.

But he just kneeled and came straight toward the shore, shouting, "Yahoo!"

Finally the wave broke and crashed. The board struck the sand and the surfer tumbled off into the roiling water with a chilly splash.

He jumped up, shaking the water out of his hair and raised a triumphant fist. "I did it!"

I felt a start.

It was Derman!

Dripping foam and seawater, he picked up the board and ran toward us.

"Did you see that?" he cried, seawater running from his hair and face. "I caught my first wave!"

"Congratulations." Andros smiled approvingly.

"My first wave!" Derman yelled again. "Awesome!"

I was stunned. This *had* to be a dream. Derman wearing a tattered wet suit? Derman Bloom *surfing?*

"You have to try this, Legs!" he gasped excitedly. "It's incredible! I love it! I can't believe I never did it before! *This* is truly a religious experience!"

"Where did you get the surfboard and the wet suit?" I asked.

Derman pointed at the fire. On the sand at the very fringe of the orange glowing light, Angie and the long-haired surfer named Tyler were wrapped in each other's arms.

It had been a long and trying day. I felt bleary.

Before he'd converted to surfing, Derman had set up his bright red two-man tent on the sand.

I tugged at Andros's sleeve and gestured toward the tent.

He hesitated and took a long look at the dark waves illuminated by the lights atop the van.

Then he took a long look at me...

Inside the tent we settled side by side, facing each other, pressed close together.

In the dark my fingers traced his stubbly jaw and fine roman nose. I felt his hot breath on my cheek.

Somewhere in Alaska, lovesick non-mating walruses were throwing themselves off a cliff.

Somewhere in Missouri a man with a beer bottle and a kitten was searching for a Tickle Me Elmo doll.

Somewhere in cyberspace a lonesome boy had just been put on bozo filter.

Somewhere in space a huge dark asteroid named after the Greek god of love was threatening to destroy us.

All around the world, people were bracing themselves for whatever was coming.

All searching for meaning.

All asking why.

But snug and warm in the arms of Andros I felt I'd found the answer.

In the absence of reason.

In the midst of chaos.

Stands the castle of love.

22

"I BELIEVE THAT UNARMED TRUTH
AND UNCONDITIONAL LOVE WILL HAVE
THE FINAL WORD IN REALITY."
—*Martin Luther King, Jr.*

I opened my eyes. The tent was filled with grayish light.

Outside I could hear the mild splash of small waves.

The air felt damp and heavy.

Beside me Andros slept in his clothes.

I slipped out of his arms and crawled outside.

The world was shrouded in mist, the sand damp and cold, the sun unseen behind a thick film of fog.

The driftwood fire smoldered, a heap of gray ash.

Around it lay surfers wrapped in sleeping bags and blankets.

Down the beach, drifting in and out of the haze, a lone figure sat beside a surfboard.

It was Derman.

His hair was stringy and matted with sand.

I walked over and sat down beside him.

The sea beyond us disappeared into the mist.

"We've been spared," he said.

"How do you know?" I asked.

"I know."

A vast wave of relief washed through me. The chained-up tension, the fear of not knowing...the knots inside me broke apart and dissolved into nothingness. I started to cry.

Derman put his arm around my shoulders. "It's okay."

"Yes, yes, I know." I sniffed and wiped my nose on my sleeve. The moment passed. Despite the thick fog, I felt as if the sun had just come out.

The dizzying glare of almost unlimited amounts of life still left to live!

The impact of there being no impact...

"I think," I began slowly, "that I just had the best last night on earth a girl could have."

"Don't rub it in," Derman grumbled.

There was something about his tone. "Wait, you don't think we..."

"Isn't that what you're implying?" he asked.

"Heavens, no, nothing like that. I may be madly in love, but I hardly even know him. Our clothes never left our bodies. I swear."

"The three rules of virginity," Derman said in a mocking tone.

"Are no concern of mine," I assured him.

"Well, hooray for small victories." Derman winked.

"Where's Angie?" I asked.

Derman jerked his head back toward the parking lot. "In her car, sleeping."

I started to rise.

"Legs?" Derman looked up at me.

"Yes?"

"Can I tell you a secret?"

I hesitated uncertainly.

Derman scowled, then grinned. He had a patch of sand on his cheek. "Not about Angie, about me."

"Okay."

"I once thought that life expectancy meant the amount of money you could expect to earn in your life," he said. "Even after I knew that wasn't what it meant, I liked to pretend it was. But last night I found a new meaning. Something better than trading make-believe commodity futures."

"Surfing?"

Derman nodded. "A sport that doesn't require good hand-eye coordination."

"I guess we can't say nothing's changed," I said.

Derman glanced back at his tent. "So what are you going to do?"

"What time is it?" I asked back.

He checked his watch. "A little before seven."

"OhmyGod!" I swallowed. "We'll be late for school!"

23

> "To live is like to love—
> All reason is against it,
> And all healthy instinct is for it."
>
> —*Samuel Butler*

"You're not serious," Derman said as he followed me up the beach.

"Of course I'm serious," I said. "Have you ever known me to miss a day of school, except for near-death illness?"

"No, but—"

"There are no 'buts' when it comes to education."

"But what about...you know who?" he asked.

I paused at the top of the dune and glanced back through the haze at the small red tent on the beach.

Oh, Andros, I thought wistfully, *Whyfore art thou?*

"Let sleeping dogs lie." I pressed onward toward the parking lot.

We reached Angie's car.

She was curled up in the backseat, asleep. Her auburn hair splashed over the beige leather upholstery.

"You going to wake her?" Derman asked.

"Where are the keys?" I asked.

"In the ignition," Derman answered. "You're going to drive?"

"Why not?"

"It's not your car."

"Angie won't mind."

We were on the road away from the beach.

Derman stared at me as I drove.

"What?" I asked.

"You're really going back to school?"

"I'm going home first," I said. "You don't expect me to wear the same clothes two days in a row, do you?"

"You're insane."

"Funny, I don't feel insane."

"You're acting like nothing happened," he said.

Just then Angie stuck her sleepy head up between us. "What happened?" she asked with a yawn.

"Nothing," I said.

"Okay." She lay back down.

We got to my house.

By then Angie was up again, and awake enough to take over the wheel. We said our good-byes.

I let myself in the front door.

No one was downstairs yet.

But I could hear footsteps above.

Slow, sleepy morning grunts.

I went upstairs and into my room.

Got out of my damp, sandy clothes.

Went down the hall to the bathroom.

The bathroom door opened and my little sister, Kara, came out bleary-eyed and scratching her head.

Without a word she passed me in the hall.

I'm not sure she even saw me.

I took a long shower.

The air in the bathroom became thick with steam.

The hot water felt wonderful.

More people use blue toothbrushes than red toothbrushes.

In the 1700s the Spanish believed that brushing with urine would make their teeth whiter.

One of the ingredients in lipstick is fish scales.

A man from South Carolina claims he was struck by lightning so hard that his shoes were welded to the floor. He says that he was dead for twenty-eight minutes, and then he came back to life. He says that while dead he visited crystal cities inhabited by light creatures. He believes that we are really light beings trapped in clumsy bodies of protoplasm, and that death returns us to our original, natural form.

Does anyone really know?

I put on clean clothes and went downstairs.

My mother and father were already in the kitchen.

Dad was buttering toast.

Mom looked up from the newspaper. "Hi, hon, sleep okay?"

"No, I was up most of the night," I answered with a yawn. "Does it say anything about the world almost ending?"

Mom turned back to the front page. There, in a big black headline as large as I'd ever seen, was:

NEAR MISS!
Huge Asteroid Almost Hits Earth!
Impact Would Have Been Catastrophic
Questions Raised About Lack of Warning
Rumor Was On Internet; Was Government Silence Right?

Mom lowered the paper and let out a long, uncomfortable sigh. "I guess I owe you an apology."

"Not really," I said. "No one knew for certain. I mean, no one except the government."

"They did the right thing," Dad said, bringing a plate of toast and a pitcher of orange juice over to the table. "Otherwise it would have been chaos. And there's nothing we could have done to defend ourselves against it anyway."

Mom actually shivered at the thought. "Could you imagine?"

"It just goes to show you," Dad said. "We think we control our own destinies. But it's all left up to chance."

"I suppose we have a lot to be thankful for," said Mom. "I mean, just the fact that we're alive."

I thought of Andros.

We ate breakfast. No one said anything. I think we were all listening to the sound of our own breaths and thinking what an amazing thing life was.

"Think you could take Kara to the orthodontist today after school?" Dad broke the silence.

"I may have to ask Angie to drive us," I said. "My car's at the beach. And I need some money."

"Sure, hon," replied Mom. "Take whatever you want out of my wallet."

Life had returned to normal.

I had to take the bus to school. The ninth and tenth graders stared at me like I was an alien.

At school I got out at the bus circle with everyone else.

But instead of going in, I walked over to the student parking lot.

The established cliques had collected in their usual tribal gathering places.

The burnouts were palming their cigarettes over by the grease spots at the far end of the lot.

The wanna-bes were squeezed in between cars, busy touching up each other's makeup.

The car freaks were huddled around someone's open hood, worshiping a new carburetor.

The jocks were ranging all over the lot, pumping testosterone and challenging everyone else's territorial rights in the guise of throwing a football.

I found Angie waiting for me by her car, looking remarkably radiant and made-up, all things considered.

The bell rang.

We fell into step with the rest of the herd, trundling toward the entrance.

"Hello, ladies." Derman jogged up, still wearing Tyler's tattered wet suit. Sand still in his hair.

Angie stiffened. "Don't forget, Derman, it didn't happen."

"What didn't happen?" Derman asked slyly. "I don't know what you're talking about."

Angie smiled and kissed him on the cheek. "Thanks, pal. I owe you one."

We got inside school. Angie headed for her homeroom. Derman and I loitered for a moment in the crowd.

Derman was the only one in school wearing a wet suit.

"Do you really have the inner fortitude to keep the secret?" I asked.

Derman shot me an ironic grin. "Doesn't matter, Legs. No one would've believed me anyway."

"What can we learn from this?" Mr. Dante asked, scratching his beard. Tiny flakes of white fell out and onto the lapels of his blue blazer.

And with that, another of life's little mysteries was solved.

24

"He spake of love, such love as spirits feel
In worlds whose course is equable and pure:
No fears to beat away—no strife to heal,
The past unsighed for, and the future sure."
—*William Wordsworth*

For so long I felt like a human TV network showing the stories of everyone around me.

But never having a story of my own.

Welcome to Allegra TV.

This was the typical schedule:

Befuddled starring Derman Bloom.

The Inane Information Minute brought to you by me.

The Beautiful and the Sexless starring Angie Sunberg.

Assisted Suicide: Pro or Con? hosted by Alice Hackett.

The Mysteries of Dandruff starring Mr. Dante.

But, thanks to a giant asteroid named after the Greek god of love, it was time to have a real show. A show of my own. I already had the title: *Life with Andros.*

* * *

He was standing at the end of the hall.

Wearing his brown leather motorcycle jacket, his motorcycle gloves tucked neatly into his scuffed red helmet.

He smiled.

I started toward him.

Just then Alice came out of the girls' room.

She looked pale and needy. "Can you believe it, Legs? The government lied! We have to talk."

"Not right now," I said.

And continued toward Andros.

FIC
STR